A DRINK TO A WORLD DOOMED

A FANTASY NOVEL

JONATHAN EVAN HUDSON

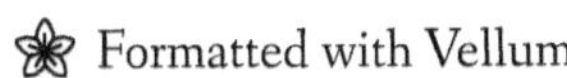 Formatted with Vellum

A DRINK TO A WORLD DOOMED

PROLOGUE

CAPTAIN DENZEL COLE, THE STERNLY DISHEARTENED

The chill in the crisp air hung over Captain Denzel Cole like an icicle about to fall.

The utter silence unfitting of the rocky mountains, all high enough for snow to cap their tops. Their bare gray slopes full of boulders and cracks big enough to hide two grown men, one standing on the other's shoulders.

More than enough cover for a small platoon of enemies to try to sneak up on the solid, fifty-foot ridge that formed the best natural barricade against an enemy army's passage across the Storm Mountains.

And called the Storm Killer.

With a pair of the most experienced archers – protected by a trio of a highly trained privates with shields, swords, and spears – all stationed every several feet along the ridge.

All three hundred yards.

Their three quivers, only one worn, each filled with two

dozen arrows. One arrow now ready to string to their long-bows. All of them wore thick dark leather armor – only strong enough to deflect the weakest of their enemy's blows.

But better than nothing.

Covering themselves with pelts of grey fur – some striped black, others blended with brown and black. The pelts of lycan. Vicious wolf men and cat women beasts of the darkness that few men could hunt down except in groups.

Sometimes.

Those who dared, who succeeded earned more good coin selling the pelts than an honest captain ever could. Normally the Princes of the Realms would never spend so heavily on their enlisted troops. Especially the commoners.

But here at the ridge things were different.

Here the pelts made clear these men didn't fear retaliation from lycan or any other darklings that dared try crossing into the Four Realms.

Until now.

The wind still refused to blow. To howl those eerie sounds that usually spooked the fresh meat.

No.

It stagnated with the smell of rancid actual meat. Of decaying human flesh.

Somehow thinned enough to be a vile peppery spice that burned all the men's tongues sour.

More than forty human skulls – each pierced high through the cap by a crude spike – formed a gruesome fence over four hundred yards away. A hundred too many yards from the ridge to knock down. Bits of bloody flesh still clung to the newest victims.

Champions sent to kill the Beast.

Champions all killed by the Beast.

Eaten by it.

Champions like Sir Torren Welsh. Once a mountain of highly trained muscles packed into the finest steel armor forged by request of Prince Wallace himself. The warrior ruler of the Eastern Realm.

And Captain Denzel Cole's highest liege.

Sir Torren Welsh, unlike so many of the champion warriors summoned by the princes, shared his drink and food with the troops on the wall. The most crisp, bitter ales. The fattest, juiciest, slabs of beef. Spoke to the troops of the Storm Killer as comrades in arms. His legendary generosity only matched by the legendary prowess he demonstrated in their friendly sparing bouts. Clearly intended to help train men beyond the limited training yet vast experience of the ridge's troops.

Till Sir Torren Welsh rode out to meet the Beast's challenge.

And lost his head only moments after the bout began.

His brain gorged out and eaten in front of everyone.

The chill that zapped the captain spine never left it since that day a month ago.

Only more champions, all just as highly trained and legendary, met the same fate. One a day. To meet a challenge by that Beast.

A daily sacrifice that kept the Beast from leading its horde of fellow monsters against the ridge.

Yet a sliver of twisted good had come into this is gut-wrenching mess. For the first time in years, Captain Denzel Cole finally understood his son's agony. His first and only son Ash. A black-haired wiry boy of fifteen three years ago. Blue eyes bright and gleaming.

Like a young Captain Denzel Cole himself.

Except softened too much by his mother. Unknowingly following the original dream of his beautiful social butterfly of a mother – to become the greatest playwright and actor in the Four Realms. His romantic shenanigans couldn't cause the captain more grief. That witty humor, striking the wrong topics too hard, would have gotten the boy jailed under a less tolerant Duke.

But that carefree youth vanished soon after the lycan raided their city. When they stole his beloved Amber – another beautiful social butterfly with the same dream as Ash. Torturing her in front of him.

While he could only watch from the top of some sturdy tall stage prop.

A flimsy wooden stick in his hand.

But throwing away his silly dreams, training like a madman under his father, Ash vanished the moment Captain Denzel Cole insisted his son use some sense. That hunting down the lycan raiders, that somehow locating, then raiding the hidden dark village Amber no doubt was enslaved in, that whole scheme was utter insanity. Amber, if she lived by then, was a broken empty shell obedient to her lycan masters.

But no.

Ash vanished.

Gone so suddenly like the captain's wife of three decades.

Both now dead from vengeance gone horribly wrong.

And a soldier's death the only thing he was now fit for.

A CRACKLE ERUPTED a few feet from the captain's side.

Loud enough for anyone on the ridge to hear. For the army of silent, unseen monsters camped out several thousand yards beyond the ridge, behind the curve in the wide passageway and hidden by one of the many snowcapped mountains, to hear.

And no wind to muddle the sound. Including when the darkling army arrived and roared in a single horrible cry.

Then fell silent.

But Captain Denzel Cole didn't need to look closely to know the source.

A private.

Hard leather boots mere inches from the deep drop of the ridge's edge. The kind of position that made most men suck in a gulp of chilled air too quickly. The cold stabbing their teeth hard. Tasting that rancid meat aftertaste strongly enough to turn their stomach nauseous.

The captain forced himself not to though.

The private stood a few feet away from his proper position. He should be beside his archer, not so far in front of him. In normal times he would have no excuse. Within the width of the walkway a solid ten feet, there was plenty of room for each small group of men. If the private was thinking clearly, coaxing the archer a couple feet forward shouldn't have been too hard.

Except the private's legs trembled visibly.

Despite the robe of gray pelts around his body. Including his brawny legs.

His chiseled face couldn't be more than twenty-five or so. What some women might find handsome. Especially with the straggly short blonde hair.

But the strain on his brow, the glassy look in his eyes – it told the captain everything he needed to know.

The captain walked over.

Let the private hear his approach.

The taste of rancid meat still too strong for him to forget the horror that would soon come.

"Seems the Beast is late," said the captain. Gruff yet gentle.

The private gulped.

Loud and wet.

And exactly what the Beast wanted.

"If the gods have any mercy at all, they won't let it come today," the private said. His voice trembling as much as his legs.

But hopefully not carrying too far.

"A wish we all have," said the captain.

Gave the private a solid pat on his upper arm.

Reminded the captain of the other troops who said something similar. How a little sympathy, some words of encouragement, did far more than the strictest discipline to get them through these moments of weakness.

Especially in such dark times.

"Then Sir Isaac won't have to fight it," said the private, his voice becoming a bit too breathless, too high-pitched, "Won't have to die like all the others."

The captain knew exactly the horror the young private feared.

His childhood hero, the one that inspired the private to enlist, to spend his best years of his life protecting the Four Realms, that very man was about to meet a gruesome, pointless doom. One that proved his strength was no better than a slug against a soldier's boot.

A sight a number of the troops here had seen since the Beast arrived two months ago.

A champion a day.

So many dreams broken.

Destroyed.

The will to fight, to protect crumbling each day.

Till everyone here accepted their pointless doom.

"Stand firm and pray," said the captain. His tone as gentle as he could manage. His men needed hope. Real hope. Not words.

Yet he would fail them just like he failed his wife.

Failed his son.

And cost more than his own worthless life. His soldiers' lives.

"That's all we can do now," said Captain Denzel Cole, "And it's best you don't let Sir Isaac hear –"

An inhuman roar broke out before the ridge.

The source a rat man so big, so tall, its height was twice the tallest of men. Its brawn so massive it could easily lift a struggling stallion – wearing the most sturdy, heaviest armor of the Four Realms– and crush it like a fragile egg. Curved claws like short daggers. Capable of stabbing through the hardest steel.

Yet its black fur was groomed neatly in spikes. Fangs larger than most trolls yet trimmed sharp and pristine white.

It's even blacker pants clean and unwrinkled. Not a speck of filth on its crimson vest with golden spirals.

Not a sign of the blood and flesh it gorged itself on the prior days.

Not even on its colossal battle axe. The wilted yellow skull engraved into the blue steel, double-sided blade. The red glowing eye sockets. Or the thick handle planted into the dirt beside him. Or the spiked tip pointing straight up toward the cloudless sky.

"Bring forth today's challenger!" exclaimed the Beast, "Do that and I grant you one more day for your menfolk to quiver in fear. For you woman to wail at their future fate as our slaves. And mourn your children before my kind roast and feast on them all!"

Captain Denzel Cole bared his teeth. The urge to the hazardous stairs carved into an exposed indent of the ridge. Throw himself at the Beast. Throw himself at the mercy of the heartless gods.

And pray for a miracle.

"Dear Gods," said the private, his voice now cracking, "Can't we try feathering it again?"

The captain bite down his foolhardy urge.

His troops needed a leader to keep their spirit from breaking. He stood even less chance against that rat monster than any of the champions. Than men taken from the fittest bloodlines. Men trained for battle since they could walk.

"Didn't do any good last time," said the captain, knowing the very same question was going through many of his troop's minds.

Despite the fact the Beast positioned itself far out of reach of their arrows.

"Won't do any good this time," said the captain.

"Ho!" shouted a burly voice.

One belonging to a giant of a man. Covered head to toe in thick plate armor. The rich golden emblems of birds engraved into the steel, combined with the precious gemstones carved into colorful flowers, marked the champion as Sir Isaac.

And striding toward the villainous Beast. Broadsword out. The blade as thick as a brawny arm and as long as a young man.

A weapon only someone as massive and strong as Sir Isaac could wield.

"I accept your challenge, foul Beast," said Sir Isaac.

The echo of his words punched the rock mountains. As if only Sir Isaac himself could smash the icicle that seemed to hang over all the troops of Storm Killer.

The champion marched straight up to the Beast.

Who merely smirked back at the human.

And waited.

Till Sir Isaac reached the last dozen feet.

And the champion charged.

His boots pounding the rocky dirt.

His armor clanking as loud as a small cavalry.

Broadsword arced out.

Ready for one critical swing.

Ready to crush the black heart of the rat monster.

The captain held his breath. His insides knotted ice. The taste of rancid meat in the air a stark reminder of failure.

Sir Isaac crossed the reach of Beast's weapon.

Continued on.

No turning back. His arm heaving his broadsword. Arching toward the rat monster's neck.

When the Beast grabbed Sir Isaac's head.

Slashed it off with its claws.

Blood gushing everywhere.

"Sir Isaac ..." whimpered the young private. Voice barely a whisper.

Yet cracking all the same.

The champion's body collapsed a moment later. The loud clang followed by utter silence.

And the Beast held up Sir Isaac's head.

Another trophy to feast on in front of the ridge's troops.

To place on a spike and taunt them with.

Until the Beast crushed it.

A mush of gore spurting out of the golden helm.

"So many champions," yelled the Beast, "Yet all so pathetic none lasted more than a moment!"

The Beast bared its giant fangs in a snarl.

"Listen up, humans!" shouted the Beast, "You get one last chance. Your next champion to fall to my claws will spell the end of your kind. The day before the next fat moon. That is the deadline."

Only three days. An impossible deadline.

Captain Denzel Cole nearly fell to his knees.

Nearly plugged his dagger into his heart.

But no.

Humanity had to go down fighting.

Just like his wife. Stabbed to death by a jealous rival over some social butterfly nonsense.

Yet she managed to fatally wound the bitch.

Just like his son Ash. Committed to die fighting the lycan bastards that destroyed the love of his life.

Just like the captain did so long ago, rescuing his future wife when a vicious rat man abducted her, ravaged and salvaged her, all because that darkling heard a rumor that she contained a seed of magic leftover from a mysterious, long forgotten lover.

Any decent soldier knew what they had to do.

And it kept the captain standing firm.

CHAPTER
ONE

ASH, THE STUPID DRUNK

Smelling the rich bittersweet aroma of spiced ale and mulled wine, the cries and stomps of a crowd still dancing wild hours passed sundown, not to forget the juicy roasts of turkey legs everywhere with minced meat pies handed out for snacks to anyone with enough hands and stomach to spare ...

As the beloved red-headed nutcase of a bodyguard called Penny loves to tell her darling life-long client Ash: behave and maybe, maybe, a girl or two might fall for you.

Maybe.

A big maybe.

Because in this crowd tapping their hearts out on the cobble streets, cramped into tight streets between two story stone houses packed into even tighter rows, Ash hoped to find maybe, hopefully, one girl sober enough, or possibly drunk enough, to actually do more than talk slurred to him.

You know, flirt, dance, and snuggle ... naked. The way Amber used to do with him way back when he was an innocent actor-wannabe defying the great retired Captain Denzel Cole.

Well, after his minor little mission tonight, of course.

The bright paints decorating every wall with images of exotic fruits, flowers, and birds suggested the city of Chemiran was a hotbed of romance, drinking, and other crazy fun. The perfect place to a girl and guy to rub naked together.

With zillions of zigzagging roads, there's plenty of places to sneak off to.

Full of more cafes, bookstores, and coffee shops than any sane people could ever need. All packed with furnished wood sculpted in curvy elegant fashions of various begone eras, from savages from foreign wildernesses to the domestic predecessors to Storm's End, from real civilizations or imagined.

Especially imagined.

Creatures so elegantly designed and curvy they could never hope to walk anywhere on their hooves, paws or whatever mutation the artist deemed they should try to walk on – as long as it was beautiful.

Columns so twisty and narrow they could never hope to support anything except a couple pieces of parchment. Marble statues of lady goddesses so beautifully proportioned with big chests and narrow waists and lush hip ratios that they had the tendency to topple over from the slightest breeze.

But Penny loved them all.

Just like Amber would of.

The way her heart of a face lit up every time Penny

stepped into a new place. Saw another of those crazy statue goddesses. Or an elegant creature built so weird no regular mortal could love. Her ruby red pony tail dancing as much as her leather boots. Not to mention how many times the guys said she was built like a wine bottle to a sober drunk.

(They were also drunk when they say it ... but clearly not sober enough to notice her sword strapped to her hips. Her orange button down shirt and green trousers tight were enough for anyone to know the truth with decent enough accuracy anyway.)

Of course, Ash discovered in a rather painful accident (painful as in Penny punching his perverted gut a good few times for not minding his own business) that her bra, even though it fit her nicely sized boobs perfectly (not that he'd never admit to her they were a bit smaller than those goddesses – forget ever speaking of Amber, ever), also did some kind of push up job on her goods to add to the appeal of looking at her.

(And never, ever dare speak of the part about her waist to hip and chest ratios were just slightly "imperfect" enough to make her a functional person that didn't topple over every-where like those statue goddesses she drooled over.)

Not that Ash complained.

About her boobs, ratios, or this city. Since, every single place offered great wines. Red wines flavored with every kind of spice, fruit, and wood imaginable. White wines too. Not that Ash was a white wine guy. Then there were the blue, green, and violet wines whose ingredients and making were trade secrets worthy of a dagger in the back.

Clearly something to avoid. Both the wine and the daggers.

Now when he meant every place offered wine, every single place actually did. Baths, clothing shops, even libraries.

Where else did not offering wine be considered out of place?

Because, Chemarin's libraries must be the only place in the world where the books all smell of fresh alcohol.

Where no one questioned the fact, Ash kept a tiny flask of liquor in his pants pocket.

Or that it contained a clear deadly liquid what aptly dubbed the Final Chug – because the alcohol's bite was so potent even a sip too much could drop you for the night and leave a massive hangover in its wake the next day.

Lesser men died from it.

Just a whiff got them drunker than a full bottle of purified vodka.

And this place was full of wonderful guys and girls capable of at least sniffing the stuff. There was a distinct chance it was a covert requirement of manhood or woman-hood here, in fact.

The very place you'd never expect the old bag of magical wrinkles that everyone called the Earth Wizard to hole himself up in either.

Against the darkling assassin who called herself Scarlet Knight, the wizard had taken a number of precautions. Nearly none of them explained to Ash, Penny, or those two partners of Ash's who were also actual real Paladins.

Unlike Penny. Who technically was only tagging along to protect Ash's sorry butt.

Even, as Paladins – warriors trained and dedicated to serve the four wizards that kept the land peaceful and happy or something like that – they were tasked with protecting him. By his own orders this time too.

Because the Earth Wizard was the last wizard of the four left.

Kinda reminded Ash of a play Amber wanted to perform way back when – except his pretend dad got it shut down. Afraid of upsetting the powers that be.

As if any playwright worth their pen and voice would give in to such crude threats.

Amber got enough crude threats and remarks from ungrateful one-night lovers to grow a thick skin. Metaphorically speaking, of course. Her real-life skin had been as peachy as fresh peach pudding. As warm and silky, too. Her blond hair as golden as the coins she loved. Especially that long lock of hair that flowed over the left side of her oval face. Giving her pouty cherry lips and puffy slim cheeks the perfect look of the classic femme fatale villain, she loved to play.

Her blue eyes like electric bolts out of the sky.

Until some monstrous beastmen called lycan deflected those playfully scornful bolts. Kidnapped her and broke her to their perverted lycan will.

Still, one day Ash would find her.

Learn the magic the Earth Wizard promised could heal her too.

But as Amber proclaimed during Ash's spectacularly

inept courting of her, "Don't think you can handle me until you've dated a few lesser women."

Plus, a smirky wink to make sure he got the right message.

Because the last couple years, after a couple failed attempts at real romance, his heart finally agreed it was time to move on and fulfill Amber's suggestion. Too late to fix Ash's on again and off again disaster with a redheaded Paladin beauty called the Bloody Rose.

She was a thousand miles away in an empire he never would step foot in for all he knew.

But tonight, Ash couldn't try to fulfill that long awaited requirement yet. Not until he fulfilled his duty to his real dad, the Earth Wizard.

But in his black suave coat and silky lavender button down, Ash got enough lingering glances from the crazy party-goers that he couldn't slip down the next two houses into the Earth Wizard's secret residence for the moment.

The shiny saber strapped to his side didn't help. Only rich guys carried them here.

Especially the arrogant minor nobles who owned less land than the typical farmer – yet held a title of nobility which, of course, entitled them to a nice piece of the taxes collected throughout the country *and* their official resident county.

But magic made the blade cut through nearly anything very easily as long as Ash held the handle tightly enough – not something any noble except Champions got – those few special warriors titled by the Four Princes of the Realm.

The fact the other three wizards were utterly destroyed,

despite being in heavily guarded towers and castles and whatever protection that they themselves had built personally or oversaw the building of – the Earth Wizard went the other way when it came to his current hideout and choose a simple stone house he bought centuries ago from some peddler of little note.

The mugs of ale and wine splashing everywhere would normally worry me more than a random assassin at the moment. It did make my shoulder cringe a bit.

Except the wizard not only waterproofed but added an auto-cleaning spell to all their outfits in the last few weeks. Including every single one of Penny's outfits. The more outrageous slinkier ones she loved to tease Ash with too – the way Amber loved to do way back when, a few years ago.

Even though Penny wasn't a Paladin.

Just his private bodyguard. Entirely by her own choice. Devoted wholeheartedly to him ever since he rescued her from the terrible fate of becoming a broken mindlessly obedient lycan slave like Amber was, somewhere.

Long before Ash ever became a Paladin too.

Long before Ash discovered the Earth Wizard arranged the whole thing without either of them knowing. Penny herself was actually a human construct – an artificial human built from magic and alchemy. Her soul as artificial as her body. Rescuing her activated her core mission to protect Ash. With her life if necessary.

Yet Ash never had the heart to tell her.

Star-crossed lovers, Amber would call the two of them.

Her play would include lots of action and heartache and comedy. Though Ash hoped they wouldn't end up dying at the end.

Or in the middle.

Of for gods' sake, the beginning.

At least in the real-life version,

Even after the Earth Wizard broke the news to Ash that he was his son. Captain Denzel Cole wasn't his father. The old bag of magical wrinkles was. Throwing in some magical tests for proof that no sane son would ever care to remember. A timely bottle or two of vodka erasing that little wrinkled horror show with a good hang over.

So Penny was here to keep his very rare progeny very safe and very much sound.

Her occasional questioning of her rather devoted yet supposedly lust less obsession with her client hard to deflect at times.

No way would Ash would risk ruining the bright gleam in those emerald eyes of hers with the truth.

So, when she stomped out of the nearest crowd, her face a peachy storm blushing with a cherry lightning of a pout, Ash darted toward his main destination anyway.

In the opposite direction.

And crashed into a wall of iron black brawn.

Felix.

His partner.

The humid night air suddenly a bit crisp and chill.

"You're late," he said. His speech as short as the curly fuzz on his head.

Somehow his outfit when he wore it, with his several extra inches of height and width, Felix came off far more god-like than those topple-ready goddesses.

And his thinned lips made him look like a war god barely holding back.

When Penny growled by my side.

"Figures you slouched off again," she said, "You're a worse bodyguard than me."

"Penny," barked Felix. The rest of the sentence clear even if unspoken.

Except to that red-headed darling.

The alcohol on her breath thick enough to make Ash a wobbling drunk.

Well, more of a wobbling drunk. His legs didn't need the encouragement.

"Oh please," she said, "That old fart needs to get out more. No wonder he doesn't have any heirs. Can't expect to find a lady if –"

Ash grabbed her hand before Felix unleashed a less pleasant solution.

"Heeey there," he said, "It's –"

She patted his cheek hard enough to count as a few slaps. Her control over her unusual strength did sometimes go awry if she got too drunk.

At least he hadn't lost a tooth.

Yet.

"The old fart needs us, doesn't he?" she asked. Slumping.

Felix grabbed her other hand.

His grip tight enough to make Penny grimace openly.

"Quiet," he said, "Or else."

He stood firm against her yank or two. Her whimper and glare confirmed her surrender.

Time to meet our scheduled execution.

EXCEPT THEIR NEXT scheduled execution wasn't the one originally planned.

The first thing that warned Ash of danger was the rhythm of the movements of the nearest dancers. Cramped in these cobble streets they all started closing in on their targets in that pretend random way you see in lesser theatrical performances too often.

Amber pointed it out regularly way back when. Scolded every actor and actress who dared marred her plays with such contrived behavior till none dared think of it.

Even in their dreams.

Those chilly sweaty wake-ups good whenever the morning was otherwise too unpleasantly warm.

None of the dancers here carried the obligatory turkey leg or minced meat pie. Forget the obligatory mug of ale or cup of wine. Their eyes more on the houses around the Paladins. Especially the slim alleys cramped between them. Most too thin for any real escape attempt.

Especially the ones closest to Felix and Ash.

They all dressed in the flashy bright colored shirts, vests, and trousers of ordinary commoners. Laughing and swinging around with a solid mix of girls and guys all rather handsome and pretty. Build like wine bottles and vodka bottles, as the Chemarin saying goes.

Except their eyes, every single one of them, were more sober, more furious than a drunk deprived of alcohol too long – and with the best selection teasing them mere inches from his face.

Their pants were baggy too. Dresses puffed out around the hips and legs. Tweed caps carefully positioned over their hair. Over the sides of their head.

But not careful enough.

Ash spotted the furry hints of wolf ears jutting out of the guys' hair. Mottled grey, brown, or black. The color of a male lycan's fur coat. The girls and their cat ears too. Orange, yellow, or blue grey. Striped black. The color of a female lycan's fur coat.

Their baggy bottoms would be hiding their tails. Wolves for the guys. Tigers for the girls.

A quick estimate put the pack at thirteen lycan. Seven wolves and five tigresses.

But there were definitely more nearby.

Watching.

In case one of their targets escaped this first wave.

"Felix," Ash whispered, only careful to watch from the corner of my eyes, "Remember that time in alley town?"

Felix didn't respond. Dragging a reluctant deadweight called Penny was slow enough.

But he definitely remembered that little training scenario

back during their apprentice days, where after a nice relaxing night of drinking contests after another mind-numbingly hard exam well done, their got ambushed by a bunch of lycan constructs sent by their bastard instructors to ruin their fun.

They only survived because the alley was so thin and narrow the lycan could only attack in front and in back. The jutting ridges of the roofs long enough to prevent an attack from above.

The full moon being bright enough to read a full scroll under helped too.

And that Felix was the foremost Champion of this generation and several past.

Lucky for them, tonight's moon was close enough to full to help the numerous lampposts dotting the street.

Especially when they entered the dimmest spot between them.

It happened in an instant.

Twenty-one pops ripped out. Worn shabby shoes exploded to reveal puffy furry paw feet. Retractable claws out digging into the cobble.

Three-inch-long claws out of their fingertips.

Fur sprouting over their bodies. Puffing up their otherwise tight tops.

Their faces now snarling. Twelve coated in wolf fur. Mottled brown, grey, and black. Or tigress fur. Orange, yellow, or blue grey. Striped black.

Yet still horribly human. Face and body.

Despite the bared fangs.

And eyes matching their bestial bodies.

Ash managed to yank out his saber just as the lycan all lunged at the Paladins.

But Felix moved first.

Against a pair of wolves in midair. Brown and grey.

His saber a wicked flash.

Slashing a brown's throat. Gutting the grey.

His expression like a black thunderstorm.

His blade, the lightning bolts to destroy these puny ragweeds called lycan.

Ash didn't compare him to a war god for nothing.

Not to be out done, Ash managed to duck just in time to avoid an orange tigress slicing his throat open.

But not to avoid her citrus breeze. Which stupidly enough, made him hesitate.

Or maybe it was the ridiculously low neckline on her fluffy green dress.

Because big boobs were big boobs, he guessed.

And Ash was a drunk guy with the wrong priorities, as his fake dad Denzel Cole, tended to say too often.

Before he could spot her again, one of her feline companions then yowled at him.

For leering at the wrong catgirl?

His own ears pounding louder than the crowd's frantic screams didn't help either.

A flash of polka dot warning him of her attack.

Training instinct kicked in.

Ash jumped back. Turning slightly away for extra push.

Just barely dodged the claws of a yellow tigress gutting

him. In a polka dot dress. Covering her body arching in a partial pounce midair.

One that covered her up to her neck.

Made an easy target to slash.

His turn powered a kick. His boot nailing the side of her gut.

Her gasp. Wide eyed yellows. Back arched.

Struck in the kidney.

Crippling her temporarily.

A quick slash ended her, toppling over a wide-eyed snarling gurgle. A reminder that the techniques Captain Denzel Cole drilled into Ash actually worked – since kitty midair gymnastics ended the life of more than one over-confident soldier.

Paladins too.

"Laaadies, laaadies," I said, "I recommend catnip rather than murder for jealousy."

Miss Citrus Kitty mewed. As loud as a furious human-sized tabby tiger possibly could. Arching toward him. Clawed fingers wringing. Eager to slice his flesh apart. Green eyes as venomous as poison ivy. Poisonous enough to sear through his clothing and skin.

And about to pounce again.

Not miss this time either, if Ash's hunch was right. His loose legs, barely avoiding a wobble or two, agreeing with his assessment.

"Do not demean us human!" she shouted, "I am Mandy Ivy of the Clawheart Clan! I will avenge Chloe for –"

"A-avenge?" Ash asked. Pausing for dramatic effect.

The sardonic twist of his lips the pinch of sugar on top.

And the kitty falling for it.

Because for the life of him, Ash couldn't help but admire her figure. Build like the finest wine bottle in Chemarin, as the locals would say. Even if they were all currently running away at the moment.

Well, running away from the lycan, at least.

His cheeks blushed way too hot for a deathmatch against a very cute but very murderous darkling.

Not just from too much alcohol either, unfortunately.

If Amber saw him now, she'd snort. Call it a laughing huff. And spear him with a playfully scornful glare out of her right eye. Her left eye, hidden under the front of her hair, would fry him unseen but not unfelt.

But if this orange tigress wasn't covered in tiger fur, snarling fiercer than a bucket of ice water tossed on black-smith's furnace full of burning coal ...

Well, no wonder his wizard father sent him a crazy cute construct for a bodyguard.

Who, by the way, was off slaughtering other lycan. Completely oblivious to her client's rather obvious yet pathetic struggle. Several lycan already crumbled on the ground by her boot. Not of drop of their blood sullying her precious leather boots.

Definitely competing in body count against Felix's.

So Ash better wrap this up before more lycan joined Miss Citrus Kitty.

"Too cute," he said, "Just purren a l-little and you're bethefinest wine bottle in the city."

Her body snapped up in surprise. The snarl on her face vanishing into a gasp of shock.

Hitting him with a warm breath full of several bottles worth of red wine spiced with the sharpest mint.

One of the strongest wines in the city. Almost as strong as decent Gin and Toxic.

And only served in his favorite hut of a caffe down this very street. Behind him, down a couple houses.

His heart didn't know whether to sink or swim.

So he risked piling the stupid with the ultra-stupid because, well, it's Chemarin and he's too drunk to fight seriously.

"Let's try something a little different," Ash said, "A drinking contest. At the Badger's Burr Table. Winner ... uhm ..."

Her gape fortified into a grim expression that spelled his doom.

Oh well. Worth a try.

The screams of the townsfolk in the street were actually getting louder. As if, instead of escaping danger, they were running right into it.

"A proper purren challenge then," she said, "Loser serves and obeys the winner unconditionally for the rest of their life. Whether as a bed warmer or as a – **hick**-*up* – a bed warmer ... I mean, a – you know what I mean."

And licked her chops.

Pointy fangs clearly showing what she meant.

"My people *will* enforce it. With their lives, human," she added, "So don't think you can run."

As if his wobbly legs could actually run.

Joke's on her.

Flexing her claws at him in that extra murderous lycan way – it made his throat so very thankful it wasn't cut open ... yet.

Maybe the joke wasn't entirely on her.

CHAPTER

TWO

SNOW, THE MISERABLE SLAVE

Hiding her furry butt in an alley definitely saved her hind tonight.

Even if this dank crack was scrawnier than a crow in a land of deathless immortals.

Tight enough to make it hard for Snow to breath.

And this place stank worse than all those chamber pots her former human masters once forced her to use *and* to scrub clean regularly, scrubbed on and on until the dull brass shined so bright that she almost wanted to keep them as stinky treasures for herself.

Almost.

The stone houses cramped together everywhere gave her little cover anyway. No hawker stands or displays or even broad tables to sneak behind.

With humans cramped together as their buildings, her

30

white fur would stick out like thorny black burs on a white fine silk dress. Nothing here would hide the natural sky-blue highlights in her fur emphasizing her feminine curves. The whole chest, waist, and hips ratio thing that made her human master leered and drooled over her would draw attention too.

Even if her masters only did it over the price her pelt would fetch – especially since she wasn't a normal tigress lycan.

Snow was a rare exotic called a fox lycan.

Proof she was from domesticated stock too inbreed for further use, according to her wild lycan brethren.

Only to be pitied and ignored as inferior by her own kind. Whether domestic or wild.

But her livestock background left her with some decent knowledge about mankind. Like the power of alcohol, despite its sweet biting aroma that made any lycan yearn for a gulp, and the stupefying effects of drunkenness on humans.

And on lycan themselves.

Or how a celebration like this meant lots of food and drink available. Meats, sweets, and alcohol. Some for free. Most for some coin. The second of which her fellow lycan rarely carried around. Their current clothing stolen off humans they killed on the way here.

Clothing they refused to provide to Snow due to her freakish appearance.

Because her pointy fox ears would poke through the soft caps their pack needed to use in their human's form – since a lycan's human transformation didn't hide their non-human ears or tail. Her long white hair with sky blue highlights too freakish for her young pretty girl face.

Nothing she said convinced them that in her human form, her crisp peachy skin and extra nice ratios would lead the humans to overlook any oddities. Just like it did back when she had to infiltrate and play social butterfly in some obscure city for a few years. Got to play the cocky brilliant playwright and actress no human ever expected a mere lycan, let alone an exotic, could ever pull off. Enjoy the affections of man both skilled at love and those less so, especially one so adorably less so she couldn't help but smile sadly for.

At least the poor sweet boy survived the final lycan raid she had been forced to unable in order to get kidnapped by her wild brethren, to escape after a mission well done.

Even here, if Snow left her fox ears and tail out for anyone to see, she could of posed as a jester of sorts. With a few balls to juggle, maybe a few more unusual items tossed in, while singing the right rowdy songs ...

As she had done in the past, humans simply laughed her off and missed the obvious darkling in their midst.

Then again, they must have known deep down Snow might of considered warning a Paladin or two of the impending assault.

If she had found one soon enough.

The fact Snow ended up swearing to serve their beloved and supposed super-fighter Mandy Ivy as her personal slave called a purren – bound by oaths Snow was tricked into taking then compelled to obey by her race's nature ...

Well, it's not like she ever had much of a choice in anything ever.

So when Snow spotted Mandy attack the tall, dark, and handsome Paladin with his legs wobbling from too much drink, her heart sank.

No way if any of the Paladins died would they ever consider sparing Snow. No matter how many humans she worked to save.

Except Mandy missed.

Something that hadn't happened in years. The wolfs that dared purren challenge Mandy all dead and rotting.

Then the Paladin cut down some yellow tigress. The one that loved yanking Snow's tail hard whenever she didn't offer to massage her paw padded feet ... or not do it well enough to please her.

Then Mandy and the Paladin started talked in slurred drunk talk ... about a purren challenge?

Snow couldn't help but smile.

Because if Mandy became a purren, Show would get a chance to be freed from her tail-munching oaths – if Snow could convince the Paladin to release her.

Until Snow heard clicks coming from the rooftops. Harsh clicking whispers of darklings closer to vicious cruel bugs than anything else.

And Snow knew she had to act.

Her hackles too far on edge not to.

Not to just to protect Mandy. Or the Paladin.

But the whole ungrateful pack.

Looking up above, Snow squinted at the warm plum pudding sky.

Between the tile ridges a couple stories above her, plenty of stars twinkled. Like the tiny bits of sugary confectionery goo that wobbled on the various cakes her former masters loved to hand out during their numerous balls and festivals.

Except the festive music in the distance now was fading. Cut off by more and more screams,

The harsh clicking whispers coming closer and closer.

All making the fur on her back stand up stiff.

Not just her fellow lycan were attacking now.

A tingle zipped through her fingers. Her best weapon – one that only her dead litter mate Scarlet had matched – was gathering like a storm inside her.

The first black blotch scuttered by. Blocking out the sky confectionery – a spidery blotch with too many distorted human parts patched in.

Spidora.

Snow raised her hands. Fingers pointed straight her first spidery target.

Ready to strike.

Her current master Mandy was too busy blabbering with that Paladin to notice Snow right now anyway. Mandy had ordered Snow stay hidden and watch her back, but never actually even implied Snow should dare dishonor her master by saving her ungrateful furry butt.

But more harsh clicks rang out.

Several on the roofs above.

A few in my alley.

And even more on the roofs nearby.

Time for a better plan.

Or else everyone here, including Snow herself, would be cocooned and sucked dry.

THREE

ASH, THE STUPID DRUNK, PART II

Ash don't know how long he stared at those evil claws flexing at him.

Strange with screams and cries ringing out everywhere of Mandy's fellow lycan kind, and Ash's own actually, getting cut down. The gurgles and moans of dying lycan and humans.

The bitter metallic stink getting so thick in the air it was like trying to breath blood and terror. The wet thumps onto the cobble street echoing across the cramped stone houses. All so loud and random no sane person could mistake them from anything but the fall of the mortally wounded during battle.

The bittersweet aftertaste of too much ale, vodka, and wines, of too many spices and fruity flavors, all dulled what normally would of made his whole body cringe. His insides roared with righteous fire to destroy these darkling monsters slaughtering his fellow party goers.

Ruining his first chance in a long time to get wyrmed too.

Wait, that last thought really shouldn't be there.

Another sign Ash was way too drunk to fight properly.

Forget the lycan.

Go more than a few houses down and he'd get lost in the maze of zigzagging streets, get mugged by a stone wall he didn't see, and collapse in the most embarrassing position since he graduated his apprenticeship and ended up naked on the front stairs of the Paladin's Academy the next day.

Long story.

No time now.

If this gorgeous heart attack of a murderous tigress wasn't just as stupidly drunk as Ash ... well, then again, he somehow in his current state was still able to appreciate the stunningly fine hip, chest, and waist ratios of a wyrming bloodthirsty catgirl darkling. With wyrming cat fur growing out of every inch of her skin.

And appreciate she had a lovely citrus smell.

Some blend of orange and lemon he really, really shouldn't be caring about as much as he did.

The fact this Mandy simply flexed her claws at him, the evil glare from her poison ivy eyes, her pointy white fangs gleaming in the lamppost light –

Yet hadn't simply sliced his throat open.

Ash was pretty impressed with her restraint.

Amber would say go for it. Strange that this catgirls's kind destroyed the girl of his dreams yet his first reaction to them now was, especially to a pretty lycan was, well, less than proper, fiery-veined vengeance.

For a Paladin, especially.

But a chance to wyrm a girl was a chance to wyrm a girl.

Even if she was a darkling whose very race was breed for vicious murder and brutal combat. Existed solely to exterminate mankind. Trim down other races for bonus points. The added feature of fur hiding combined nice body builds matching human ones, especially the feet turning human during the fur hiding, it helped them blend in with the very races they sought to annihilate.

The fact they stood glaring at each other ...

Had Ash trusted his arms more than his wobbly legs, maybe he could of sliced her throat open right there. Or cut through a vital spot. The magic sharpness of his saber would doom her, slicing through claw or limb, unless her speed allowed her to dodge –

A speed well beyond amazing.

Simply drawing Felix's attention would do too. He was like a tornado of iron brawn cutting down lycan. Like a tornado of wind and hail cutting down rover camps.

Okay, rovers hated when people said that.

But it wasn't Ash's fault they set of a bunch of ply wood tents in the middle of vast regions of tall swaying grasses called Tornado Plains during the nice and warm and rainy time called Tornado Season and then wondered why so many tornados struck them.

Something involving a god or goddess or something, last time Ash checked.

Probably one dressed in their baggy drab clothes and

heckling worshippers to spare a coin – and not the ten the divine asspicker just pickpocketed you for.

"Well?!" growled Mandy. Her claws freezing in a sinister curled up gesture.

And Penny, his devoted nutcase of a bodyguard, now a few dozen feet away, was still engrossed in slaughtering as many lycan as her new nemesis rival, Felix the War God.

The cuts over her body already being to heal.

While he hadn't received a scratch yet.

Never mind Felix was the foremost Champion of this generation and many several prior.

That these poor murderous darklings were feeling was his pent-up fury at the wizard forbidding him from running up north to face down a ratling's grand challenge at the Storm Killer. One that would define his generation and many to come.

"Uhm, what?" Ash asked. Then stumbled out the rest. "Was the question?"

His throat was as good as slit.

But she actually barked out a laugh.

"So you do know the proper method of a purren challenge," she said. Her grin said he was a mouse worth playing with alive.

So far.

"I," she said, "Mandy Ivy of the Clawheart Clan, do challenge you ..."

His heart hit a wall.

Another test?

But his drunk mouth spat out his name before his brain could stop it.

"Ash La Pushka," he said.

His real name.

With the very well known and very unique surname of the one and only Earth Wizard.

The glint in the catgirl's poison ivy eyes became clear enough to shout that she connected the bucket to the water.

If Ashe survived, his dad would kill him.

No.

The old bag of wrinkles would just laugh at his face. Call him wet behind the ears.

Felix would be the one to kill Ash.

Followed by a thorough stabbing by Connie, his other Paladin partner. She was currently trapped guarding the old bag of magical wrinkled while he did his scholarly thing in his secret home away from home.

Mandy's claws retracted. Chilling Ash's blood colder than a blizzard high up above tree level, up in the mountain passes Paladins sometimes trained in during their later apprentice years.

Her grim expression even more serious.

And her words more solemn.

"To a drinking contest for disrespecting my clan and insulting my clan sister, after taking her life," she said, "I demand the loser to our match serve and obey the winner unconditionally and loyally for the rest of their life."

"I ... uhm," Ash said. His mouth not happy with his mind

blanking at this very moment for no good reason other than too much alcohol. "Well ..."

"Just say *yes*!" she snapped.

"Yes," he said.

Before Ash could think about it.

Before he noticed Felix and Penny had almost wiped out the nearby lycan. Were positioning themselves to chase down the darklings hidden by, and cutting down, the screaming panicked crowds in the distance.

Both too focused, too confident on Ash's competence while too drunk, for either to notice his rather pathetic predicament.

When Felix glanced at him.

Rolled his eyes.

And preceded to ignore him.

Ah, Ash was crow bait.

That sign technically meant Felix approved Ash's rather desperately idiotic "plan" to defeat Mandy by alcohol rather than the common methods normal sane sober fighters used.

That Felix recognized this crazy plan might reveal more info on the true enemy behind this attack, uhm, well. Maybe it might give the good guys a chance to learn a few of the many deadly secrets lycans refused to speak of. You know, despite centuries of interrogators from every kingdom torturing them to the worst deaths possible at some point or another, Ash might happen to capture the one lycan that would break.

Uh huh.

Which was why out of all the murderous darklings in the world, the professionals feared the lycan the most.

Out of all the darklings in the world, they were the only ones who choose always the worst agonizing deaths rather than betray either their clan, honor, or oaths.

And their coming of age oath was to exterminate the human race.

CHAPTER

FOUR

SNOW, THE REBELLIOUS SLAVE

With her current master and the dark, tall, and handsome Paladin strolling away like drunks determined to get even more drunk, Snow knew she had little time to spare before the spidora launched their assault from the rooftops.

Little time left to change their path.

The harsh clicking whispers even more numerous now. Right above her. More echoing in this alley.

All full of buggy bloodlust.

And even more on other roofs.

The screams of humans in the distance becoming even louder.

More desperate.

Making her shoulders cringe of the thought of their horrible deaths.

Got her to gaze back up at the warm plum pudding sky between the tile ridges.

The kind of warm summer sky Snow once long ago yearned to lay down under. Hidden in a grassy field and slurp up a bowl of stolen pudding while watching for a falling star to grant her foolish wish for freedom and a careful fun life.

A life she pretended so have those years ago as an actress and playwright.

Not get stuck in this cramped alleyway between two stone buildings. The stone was like an oven finally cool enough to touch.

Barely.

But she spotted several more spidery blotches of spidora. Blocking out huge chucks of the twinkling confectionery stars.

Their poses arched. Ready to strike.

Her hands arched up. Fingers out and all pointed at them.

The humans in this city would of accepted her. Probably. In her human form. Snow came off as a pretty enough girl that the guys would overlook the foxy parts with any plausible excuse – like being cursed or something – since everyone knew lycan females were tigresses, not vixens.

As long as Snow didn't show off her furry covered ass form too soon.

Because beautiful girls did get cut more slack than any other being alive.

Except possibly, sometimes the most adorable children – mostly only by their own parents too.

Still, this cramped alleyway didn't give Snow enough room to attack the spidora properly. The jagged bolts of her electric ice blast would hit the stone walls. Diminish her attack's powers.

Maybe get a few large rocks landing on her for her efforts.

The stone against her back was hot enough for this humid summer night to make her want to pant out loud constantly. Like being squished inside a baker's oven.

Or being roasted by ratling.

But the spidora above Snow could never fit within this scrawny alleyway.

So, what was making the harsh clicking whispers down here?

It's not like the lycan village that decided it had captured Snow, rather than retrieved her from a mission well done, ever bothered to train her in any kind of combat. Basically, they decided enslave her as a purren rather than treat her as a fellow lycan returned home. The exotic fox lycan thing made Snow a trophy to show off. Not much other use.

Especially since she never revealed her magical talents to anyone.

Ever.

Even Mandy thought of her more a burden – except she had some unusually useful healing skills.

Which were actually magic. But Snow hid that part well enough.

Too well.

Even if being a purren was better than their typical human slaves. At least, purren had some rights.

Rights the other lycan made a point to enforce, in fact.

Way better than the fate of other slaves.

Still, Snow could never defeat this horde of spidora about to annihilate the lycan, humans, and me with only her magic.

At least not directly. Not without undoing her subtle, weak, but massive spell that helped hide the humans inside their homes from by subduing their human scents, heartbeats, and other giveaways.

Her back still tingling and itching from being roasted by rock ...

An idea made her ears perk up painfully.

Stone conducts heat really well.

Too well.

Her stays in castles, full of stone and chilly drafts, in order for her human master to show her exotic fox ass off to the highest bidders taught Snow stone conducts the cold as good as the heat.

So she changed the target.

And let off that first blast of electric ice.

The jagged streaks blasted out like sky blue lightning bolts.

Zigzagged through the air.

And mushroomed out like the fountains that nobles loved in their courtyards.

Striking more tiles and roofs than she could count.

Freezing them so cold they cracked louder than all the screams in the distance put together.

The shrieks of spidora hit. Their exoskeletons cracking apart. Their violet gloop splattering everywhere.

And the gloop crystalizing.

Confirmed by the crackle of small crystals raining down on the ice.

Then more of both sounds as more spidora realized their legs had frozen with the tiles.

Yet still tried too hard to move.

Shattering them.

But the harsh clicks in the alleyway echoed even louder.

More urgent.

And far too close to strike with any of her magic.

So Snow shoved herself out of this cramped stinky crack between buildings.

And spotted one of the Paladins watching her from the corner of his eyes. A massive mountain of dark human brawn that had piles of her fellow wolves and tigresses lying dead and dying around him.

Yet he merely gave me a thankful nod and motioned for her to flee.

Unnoticed by the feisty redheaded human girl near him. Who also had plenty of lycan corpses around her too. Her sword dark with blood just like the Paladin and his blade.

Her heart lifted for once in her life.

And she mouthed, *Thanks, I'm Azura Snow.*

He actually replied.

Out loud.

"Azura Snow," he said, "I'm Felix Stormbringer and we are in your debt. If you encounter another Paladin, mention my name and the honor of Crow Valley to make good on it."

Snow blinked.

Heart frozen.

"If I wasn't tricked into becoming a purren ..." Snow said. Then cut off.

Whining never solved anything.

Even the pigtailed redheaded looked at Snow with some sympathy.

"Whose?" asked Felix. His grim expression clear on his intentions.

Another reason why her failure to warn them in time made her inside wrench.

At least he realized her horrid oaths prevented her from revealing too much.

"Mandy Ivy's," Snow said.

Yet suddenly he smiled a touch.

It somehow brightened the scene of death around him

"The tigress that left with Ash, right?" Felix asked.

Snow nodded.

"Then ask Ash for your freedom," said Felix, "When the time is right ... and let him know I requested it too."

That dropped her jaw.

But he continued.

"Better go and catch up to them," he said, "Hurry before you lose your chance ... Ash's drinking prowess is legendary. Even here."

Snow could only nod. Ears perking up with her tail.

Chemiran *was* the drinking capital of the Four Realms.

So she ran in the direction that her current master went.

That citrus scent too easy to pick out among all this blood and death.

CHAPTER

FIVE

ASH, THE CRAZY STUPID DRUNK, PART I

It was disturbingly too easy for Mandy to lead Ash away from the pitched battle between lycan darklings, a Champion, and a Champion wannabe.

The cobble road around his companions was full of bloody lycan corpses. A few moaning and groaning, twitching here and there. The stink so sharp and hot Ash finally sympathized with a fish struggling through a pond of scummy copper.

There was enough blood to leave a layer of liquid between the cobble as deep as a regular solid rain shower.

But from the thunderstorm called Felix. Tearing through lycan Mandy must have known just as well as the tigress Ash cut down.

Yet she merely led me away. Not a glance back. Her poison ivy eyes no longer burning so fierce either.

49

Just marching down toward to Badger's Burr Table a few couple houses down.

Probably.

Hopefully.

The occasional body of an innocent human lay here and there.

Okay, more than the occasional body.

But always in the dimmest areas. Where the lampposts didn't light their face well enough for Ash's drunk eyes to make out their features. Well, as long as he didn't look too closely at them.

Which he made an effort not to.

Because Ash knew what this time an alcohol-induced black out would cost. The lost memories of all of these humans.

Plus one vital city-saving oath.

Each stone house they passed had the doors shut. Windows shuttered.

The inside silent.

As if the folk inside were unaware lycan could easily smell them out from here.

According to his dad, both dads actually, a lycan's sense of smell matched tracking dogs. Some even rivaled blood hounds. The zillions of scents within this city wouldn't throw them off. From minced meats pies, alcohols of every sort, to roses, coffees, and the spiciest of spices, cayenne death pepper – a local variant of cayenne so strong it's killed lesser men who tried it.

Literally.

Yet Mandy strutted tall and proud. Not fazed a bit by so many hidden humans.

Knowing full well she could easily slaughter any human who dared challenge her.

Except for the extra sway of drunkenness hidden by her slightly extra stiff movements. The kind of movements some of his fellow all-too-sober Paladins achieved when Ash finally lured them into taking a sip of liquid courage ... and they ended up downing a few too many bottles ... and their training to hide wounds and weaknesses kicked in.

Still, a darkling that could appreciate the pleasures of wine enough to halt her murder spree?

Maybe lycan did have some hope after all.

One day.

Her paw feet's claws clicking and scrapping on the cobble too long – she was way more drunk than she realized.

Which was his only hope.

That and she didn't suffer an alcohol-induced memory loss after Ash won.

A hope that died a quick death the moment she turned right in front of the twin doors of Badger's Burr Table. Their design left a wide curvy arrowhead gap a few feet above any but the tallest human patron's head and a couple feet below the knees.

And prevented barring them in any meaningful way.

Those two gaps that spilled the same amber ale light into the street every other night.

Meaning the set of steel sheets only reachable by a ladder hadn't been pulled down by the headknocker Grunts yet. Given the whole process was a crazy loud and slow despite his body being built more like a massive powerful troll than a human.

Mandy shoved her way inside.

Ash quickly followed.

The square room was nothing quite as he expected it.

Of course, it was still enclosed by stone painted with silly scenes of animals of every sort going on picnics with tea and sandwiches. The round oak tables furnished as brown as the evening's burnt coffee all were still aligned in neat criss-crossing rows. Four chairs to a table.

Each.

But human sized cocoons of white silk hung at varying heights from the ceiling. Some even as low as the brass lamps jutting out the wall, still full of burning oil too.

Yet the tables were all filled with as many bottles of wine, vodka, and whiskey as the wall shelves behind the counter in back. The biting sweet aroma of alcohol flavors with spices, fruits, and candies of every sort still going strong. Even with the flat long divider of furnished oak for the bartender streaked with blood.

Bright red and fresh.

Instinct kicked in and Ash grabbed Mandy's wrist before reality nipped in.

Her hiss louder than a rattlesnake at his touch. Ash should of expected it too.

When a loud bang rang out behind them.

THE STEEL SHEETS now closed off the most obvious escape route.

Weighted down by a huge cocoon that could only be poor Grunts. The smell of cobwebs and slimy mushrooms more stomach churning than a bottle of vodka chugged down in an instant. Only feet away Ash could make out the individual silk threads.

All so tight and thick no one could ever hope to breath under it.

Ash didn't even hear him struggling.

The skin of his back cringed all the way to the nap of his neck.

Mandy's guarded crouch suggested she wasn't in on this ambush. Darklings were known to turn on each other. The fact Ash and Mandy walked into Badger Cuff Table together calmly only sealed both their fates.

The shuttered windows could be broken by the oak chairs.

Maybe.

Both were furnished. Made of solid, good quality old oak. The locks on the windows more than iron latches. They were full-fledged iron locks framing the whole shutter to keep out thieves.

Assuming they had time to dash the few feet to Mandy's side to the nearest one.

Fortunately, Ash had forgotten to return his saber to its

sheath. A stupid mistake, normally, for an idiot drunk like him.

But the drinking contest would have to wait.

Rescuing the civilians here came first.

So he began slicing through the cocoon. The sticky threads tried to cling to the edge. The slimy smell of cobwebs in moldy leaky attic growing even worse.

But his saber's cutting edge made quick work of it.

Until Mandy grabbed his wrist.

Her poison ivy eyes gave him a deep – but not quite as venomous – look.

Followed by a shake of her head.

His heart sank like snake oil in water. What kind of darkling did this? His dad, the Earth Wizard, spent so much time lecturing Ash on various random stuff he tended to forget it soon after the wizard spoke.

Definitely a habit Ash was regretting at the moment. Another wet behind the ears remark if he ever happened to mention it, though.

He was about to ask her when a wet chuckle erupted behind us. By the counter.

They jumped.

Faced it together.

It was a huge four-foot black tarantula of spiky hair on the bottom. The kind that killed by giving its victims heart attacks by popping up in unexpected places. Death by surprise, in other words. No need for its fatal venom most of the time.

But instead of a proper mouth with mandibles dropping steaming venoms, a wiry human torso stretched a good six feet or so out the top of where its spidery head should be. Skin violet and glistening like an insect's shell.

Yet its exoskeleton had exquisitely well-defined detail of its supposed brutish muscles. A head too much like an oval stretched high and jutted chin on the bottom. Bald except for the zillion red spider eyes all focused on us. Its mouth a mix of human and spider, complete with mandibles.

And clicking in drooling steaming excitement.

The hiss of each drop hitting the stone floor. Each added a bitter stink worse than a shot of concentrated vinegar and rotten lemon. Stung his nose, his eyes worse than a hundred bee stings.

Its four arms with hands with dagger fingertips – and holding a black scimitar in each.

All its blades on guard and ready to slice them both to bits.

"Ho!" said the spider darkling. Its voice half hisses, half clicks and all venom. "More meat for my – ah, it that you?"

Its zillions of eyes blinked at once. Targeted Mandy with a leer better reserved for fat juicy flies.

Her claws shot out. Every three inches of those deadly amber razors.

And for once, they weren't aimed at Ash.

A step up in life.

"It is!" it exclaimed, "The so-called best of the lycan generation, the Ivy Reap! So drunk you can hardly stand. No wonder *he* is so upset at you. The boy ... *this* boy?"

Its zillions of eyes slimed every inch of my body. If Ash was a chick, this guy was would be the kind of creep he'd slap the head off on principle. Then run his sexy pert ass off the other way for the next few hours.

Lucky for Ash, he could use a saber instead. Cut out the need to run away too.

Except his legs decided to wobble again. Right at the moment. The little damn traitors.

So Mandy decided to up end Ash's stupidity. The fiery glint returning to her poison ivy eyes – a bit too dull from drink.

She grabbed her dress' low neckline and gave it a huge yank. Ripping the whole dress in two.

Revealing further proof that she really was built like a wine bottle of the rarest and best kind.

Ignoring the tiger fur all over her body, of course. Her paw-ish feet too. And the huge razor claws. Or her twitching tiger tail.

Revealing her legs wobbled as much as mine too ... alcohol induced stupidity was definitely not limited to the human race.

"He's mine, spidora stick hole," she said, flexing her claws even more evil at the spider darkling, "*I'll* cret the gedit for capturing him. *Alive.*"

Uhm, you mean, get the credit, right Miss Citrus Kitty?

But the words that came out of his own mouth were, "W-wait, Mo Kita, credit hick stole?"

Okay, his mouth only meant to say, "Spidora?"

But that's the fun of being around a drunk. Especially in life and death situations against a darkling renowned for its innate sword mastery and cruelty, renown despite its actual physical form wasn't exactly as well known. Where the likelihood of either of them surviving keep dropping every time they opened their dumb mouths.

Every time they did something ever stupider than before.

Right now, Ash put chances of living somewhere only at abysmal – judging from his gut knotting as much as from the alcohol in it as it from actually dying.

Well, dying *before* it finished with the alcohol in it.

They had a bit more stupid to go through before their end was utterly assured.

Thank the gods.

The sudden clicks above – they might not get the chance.

Exactly why Ash didn't gamble.

Much.

Because unless you had a trick up your sleeve, always gamble on the house winning over the long run.

"Oh fuuuck it," I said, "Just let me have one more before I die."

And snatched the nearest bottle of vodka. Dead Man's Run. Chosen for its clear tall yet wide glass bottle. Showing it had only been lost a quarter of its deadly contents before its previous owner met his untimely end.

The potency so strong just the vapor could knock out the uninitiated. Even with the cap still on, it brought tears to his eyes.

Not quite anywhere near the potency of Final Chug, but Ash didn't trust his hand to find his pocket right now.

A few blinks streaked the cold drips down his cheeks as he snapped the cap off. His lips kissed the opening.

Like kissing the bottom of a dwarf's furnace at full blast.

Lifted the bottle for a chug.

But last minute, decided to flung it straight up instead.

A slice and crack meant the bottle got cut.

The twin screeches of utter agony above. Clearly, the two spider darklings had just learned a vital lesson in life.

Never spill alcohol in your eyes.

Especially not potent stuff like Dead Man's Run.

When taps and rips and bangs starting erupting everywhere on the ceiling. Meaning those spiders were running about bumping into everything, Ash began to question the wisdom of drinking another bottle of Dead Man's Run.

Then groaned.

Above him the spidora were screeching their death cries. Crashing into planks, cocoons, and stone pillars. Acting as crazy as otherwise healthy chickens certain their heads had been chopped off.

Okay, he knew Dead Man's Run was strong but this was ridiculous.

So he waved his blade at the pathetic wimps.

"Hey, crybabies!" he shouted, "Come on! It's not that bad!"

Because no way stuff he put inside himself on a regular basis was *that* bad.

Yet they chose at the moment to detach from the ceiling and crash into the floor. Turning themselves into quiet lumps of ugly twitchy spider parts right in front of the last spidora.

Disturbingly enough, their violet skin even had a few cracks. Seeping dark blood, the color of crushed blueberries.

The stink as bitter as a mouthful of unripe blueberries. Another reminder from back in his pre-apprentice days – when he wandered thick tangled woods all by his ignorant self, not to stuff just anything he fought in the woods in his mouth despite his stomach's demands, no matter how edible and tasty it looked.

Or else his bowels might end up protesting it greatly soon afterwards.

Both remaining darklings looked at Ash as if he was way more dangerous than his wobbling legs clearly demonstrated.

Better play it for all its worth.

Keeping his saber pointed at the fallen crybabies seemed a good starting point.

"Two down," he said, "One to go. Mandy Pandy, will you do the honor? I suggest the bottle to your left. The red sparkling one with a green label –"

Rasps rang out above Ash. Silk threads shifting everywhere. Straining.

Not yet breaking.

The first and last remaining spidora hissed. Cracking its mouth wide with a crazy sly grin. All four blades raising.

Its eight spider feet bending for a leap.

"My hatchlings hatch soon," it said, "A worthy meal you two will be when I dice you into –"

An explosion blew in the shutters next to Mandy. Shattered those thick oak panels.

Flinging those now jagged iron frame right at the last spidora

Who, with a whoop, sliced it in half, two blades cutting it

quick. The other two shoving the two halves clear of the spidora.

"Ivy!" called out a girl, "Out here!"

Ash started to open my mouth to ask if Ivy referred to Mandy.

Before recalling the conversations –

Mandy snatched his forearm –

"You first," she grumbled. Humanish kitty nose wrinkling.

And flung him at the open window.

Through it.

That her ridiculous strength sent him air born ... his scream should of came out more than mere wimpy "Uhm ..."

But he did manage to mimic an arrow. Sort of. The best he could, anyway.

Her aim was true.

He wished he could say the same for his.

But the crash and flops against hard jagged cobble left his limbs too bruised and achy to claim otherwise.

Flopping like a flounder on the ground. On very cold, very hard cobble. Thankfully he didn't hear any of his ribs crack. The pain suggested they were only bruised, maybe possibly fractures, but not actually broken.

Even more thankfully – his saber stayed in his hand. Somehow. Just it landed away from him.

Near his face.

But better than serving raw skewered Ash delight.

A few screams, yowls, and mews later, there was a solid thump and tap on the cobble by his feet.

So Mandy managed a more dignified escape.

"Running so soon? My hatchings will hunt you down, Ivy Reap. You and your Ash La Pushka!" laughed the spidora inside, "Just pray *he* doesn't catch you first!"

Someone yanked Ash to his feet.

But he didn't need their help to run.

Okay, okay, just a little, very welcome help.

SIX

GORDACK, SCHEMING MASSACRE, AND DINNER

Through his hexed spyglass of blood-stained bronze, Gordack surveyed Chemarin, the sprawling city of stone and cobble, from atop of the thousand-foot cliff of solid rock overlooking the place. Scanning the messy maze of tightly packed streets and scrawny short buildings soon to be rubble, he grinned at the panicked lightlings screaming for help from his darkling hordes.

Breathing in the warm fresh air, the smell of blood and death welcomed his finely trained nose and discriminating tongue.

Made his stomach yearn for the taste of roasted human based in blood gravy.

The lycan packs slaughtered plenty of their human nemesis without mercy or pause. Yowling like the beasts they were. Their claws shredding the human's puny fabrics and overpowering their wimpy resistance. Their twisted expressions showing every ounce of yearning to feast on human flesh raw. Drink the blood fresh and hot as it squirted out of their dying prey's necks.

But Gordack did give one thing to the lycan. The coppery taste of fresh hot blood was better than the dull lightling drink called wine.

Even better when the two were combined in proper proportions.

His fellow ratlings, giant rat warriors big in muscle and brain, as clever and resourceful as their smaller four-footed brethren, herded the lightling enemy properly. Directing them through the incoherent tunnels and canyons these humans called streets. Slaughtered them easily. Driving the panicked survivors toward another pack of ratlings, who patiently waiting for their change to slaughter and finish off the enemy.

The human's few feeble attempts at fighting back with their tiny daggers, fists, and sharp sticks useless.

It only made them easier to chop down.

Because, unlike their stupid lycan counterparts – or any of the other darkling races aiding in the battle – each ratling wore thick solid steel armor as dark as their fur. An axe and sword in each hand sized to match their seven to eight feet in height. Each forged to handle the strength of their huge powerful limbs.

And as sharp as their trim black claws.

Those bags of human flesh were as dead as penned livestock. Fit for eating. Roasted alive was best. Better than any pork that wander those streets.

Especially with the smell of blood and death as thick as the gravy made from their blood and fat.

His stomach groaned at the thought of simmering the blood drenching the cobble street. Put it all in a giant iron pot and put it over a fire for a few hours till it congealed into a gelatin. Spice it every half an hour with the right cyanides for that strong bitter taste that no almond could match.

That few races could stomach without an agonizing death. Lightling or darkling.

Gordack licked his chops. His two brothers stationed on opposites sides of the city. Using the classic pincher move to kill enough lightlings for the Darkest Third, the Third Greatest Lord of Darkness, to make his move. Even if the only lightlings in this city were humans, the Darkest Third titled the Soul Magus would savor every corpse, whether lightling or darkling, when he decided to arrive and use all of them to create monsters worthy of the Darkest One, the Greatest Lord of Darkness.

Use them to draw out the only wizard still left alive.

The lonely worm dubbed the Earth Wizard.

The only lightling being powerful enough to counter the Darkest Lords' plans. The other three wizards destroyed by some crazed yet powerful lycan witch – her very existence, her very power, an oddity few knew about or dared speak of openly – her potential supposedly high enough to risk destabilizing the current ranks of the Darkest Lords.

Yet the very lycan witch who would of gained the most by the insane hope of the Four Wizards. The hope for peaceful coexistence between all races.

Now crushed beyond repair.

By the very lycans who needed it the most.

Or, more accurately, would soon need it the most.

When Gordacks' spyglass landed on a disturbing sight.

A giant dark-skinned human crushing his darkling enemies like a tomcat exterminating pinkies. His build as brawny as a full-grown midget of a ratling. He even wielded it, like his blade, as skillfully and deadly as any of the three Butcher Brothers, including Gordack himself.

And for one of the Butcher Brothers to think of such thoughts, let alone their leader, of complimenting a human's fighting prowess ...

Then a red-haired girl popped into his view. One that both humans and ratlings would call small in the right places and big the better places — but toward different kinds of appetites. Her peachy skin and delicate physique made Gordack's tongue moist.

Despite her clear fighting prowess nearly matching the dark skinned human ... a single ratling feast worth butchering the city — just to obtain a single bite.

The fat in those breasts, the lean tender meat in her thighs, the savory marbled meat in her torso ...

Gordack Ubellich, the Greatest of the Butcher Brothers, the Commander General of the Darkest Third's hordes would pursue that prize personally.

When his spyglass caught sight of something even more disturbing.

A human boy, dressed the same as the dark-skinned man, ran alongside a lycan tigress. Not from her.

But like companions fleeing a mutual foe.

A tigress he recognized instantly. One both humans and ratling would call even better than the red headed girl if she were sweet tasty human rather than a bittersweet, bordering on gamey, lycan.

And the very same Ivy Reap the lycan showed off to him before this battle. Had bragged to him about as this generation's greatest fighting lycan.

Behind them was an even more disturbing sight. Something that made his fur stand on edge.

A lycan female unlike the wolves and tigresses. A white vixen. Fox ears and tall. A coat with streaks of light blue in choice spots. Highlighting her chest and other feminine curves, as the humans would say. Or the most tasty bits in a pot, as Gordack and his brothers would say. Her coat was definitely more lush than any wild lycan ever was.

And a lycan none of the other lycan had bothered to mention to him. Their biting sweet beast stinks had suggested their only thought was their victory was absolutely guaranteed.

But nothing was guaranteed in war.

Any ratling who gained rank and kept it learned that lesson early and quickly.

So Gordack twisted his spyglass. Magnified it further onto the white vixen.

Eyes as blue as the northern skies. Warm as the sun.

And made the fur on the nap of his neck tingle.

"Black Fang," growled Gordack, "Who is the white vixen that befriended the Ivy Reap?"

The black furred lycan slipped out of the shadowy boulders several feet behind and beside Gordack. Right where Gordack permitted him to hide. Built wiry, feral yellows eyes, and a master at poisons, daggers, and claws, two of which lined thick belts along his hips and chest, that lycan Black Fang preferred the empty shadows and the "dishonorable" approach of killing an enemy by any means most efficient rather than the idiotic challenge and "honorable" battle other lycan insisted on.

Including his three idiotic lycan guards assigned for too many years to guard their great General Commander. Two black wolves too chewy looking to feast on except in emergencies. And an orange tigeress too scrawny without the right curves to make her worth the effect to catch, let alone munch down, unless, of course, food got scarce enough.

Really scarce. Assuming she didn't die sooner.

The lot of them lingered in the boulders. Avoiding Black Fang, like usual. His very presence an insult to their faces.

For their single failure to stop Black Fang, a mere insult was more than merciful.

And just a temporary solution. No point wasting their lives with a swift meaningless death just to grant their corpses some measure of honor.

No. A better punishment would make their agonizing deaths useful.

And like all lycan, Black Fang was bound by any oath willingly spoken uncoerced.

Including that crazed oath reducing any lycan to a mere slave they called purren. That their idiotic race tossed such oaths around so freely, it amazed Gordack they all hadn't been enslaved by their betters already.

But Black Fang's death would come too. Someday. More painful than any other before him.

"Purren! I asked you a question!" snapped Gordack. Knowing the rules and customs of inferior races did come in handy so often.

Whether darkling or lightling.

Otherwise, Gordack would of had to kill this lycan assassin long ago, after the fool attempted to cut his throat after a failed attempt on Gordack's life. The first pathetic step was gifting the general with the fresh body of a lovely human slave girl and poisoning her roasted flesh with arsenic in the blood gravy.

A gift the Darkest Third also ended up enjoying far more than the lycan assassin ever thought possible.

A way that Black Fang never forget, judging by his glossy yellow eyes and bitter scent every time he spotted the result of his gift after the Soul Magus experimented on it.

Every time the gift now smirked down at him.

"Azura Snow," rasped Black Fang. His harsh voice a reminder of Gordack's mercy and ruthlessness. A punishment of the lycan selecting and chugging down his most corrosive poison diluted only just enough to prevent damaging his future usefulness to his new master.

A punishment that clearly wasn't enough anymore.

Gordack snarled. Careful not to make too much noise and reveal his position on the peak. "More than a name, purren. Tell me what you know of her and her kind."

"Little I know," Black Fang said, the lack of fur rustling against his belts a signal he hadn't even cringed – another sign he needed another punishment soon.

"Tell me what you *do* know," said Gordack, "And what you suspect. Make clear which is which, too. I dislike dishonest subordinates."

And disliked traitors enough to eat them alive. Their flesh not as tasty. Their blood fresh and hot was too coppery and messy.

But it sent the right message every time.

Gordack turned his spyglass' focus onto the boy with the Ivy Reap. His outfit did truly match the dark-skinned man with decent fighting prowess.

"She was breed in the pelt farms far down south," said Black Fang, obviously choosing his words too carefully, "Rumor has it a few new breeds of tamed lycan good for pelts have emerged in the farms. Breeding out what makes them lycan. Turning them into little soft pets eager to mimic and obey their breeders. Snow's time in the village ... I heard ... showed her more spoiled than the youngest of cubs. She even chooses to be the Ivy Reap's purren for life rather than prove her womanhood as a lycan. A decision, rumors say, both question the wisdom of now."

"Wisdom?" asked Gordack, "A single dark-skinned human man below has slaughtered over several dozen of your best trained warriors. A soft, farm-bred lycan might realize her lack of battle prowess compared to her wild brethren and latch onto a sympathetic master with great combat potential."

Yet Black Fang chuckled at such an obvious conclusion.

Unaware his arrogance was the very same reason he now served a better darkling as a mere slave.

Unaware of the boy now with Ivy Reap and her purren was a key target.

"A great potential?" asked Black Fang, "Snow has command of powerful elemental magics few other are even aware of, including her own master. Had she not forfeited her freedom, had she bothered to try training her body at all, she could of easily become the greatest of her generation."

And too great a threat merely to send Black Fang then.

At least in his current state.

Time to test one of Gordack's experiments. Created by the magical talents the Soul Magus had instructed Gordack on personally.

The General Commander slipped out a black glass vial containing the tiny undead parasite, built from many of the choice bits of various worthy enemies – a few of the best parts from Gordack's combat instructor and once master challenging the Champions at Storm Killer.

It would induce the needed changes in any living being foolish enough to consume it.

Induce the right mindset too.

"Black Fang," said Gordack, holding the vial out, "Take this and –"

A chuckle broke out. Smooth and milky like blood mixed with the purest cream.

Right behind Gordacks.

Sending his fur up even if he knew better than to jump or shiver.

"My beloved general," said the Soul Magus, "No need to waste your precious creation on a mere assassin dog. Better reserve it for a proper target ..."

The Darkest Third's pale finger, on a deceptively human hand, pointed right at the least expected lightling to target.

A suggestion, command really, that tasted better than any roasted human in blood gravy.

Even better than the red-haired girl it guaranteed Gordack would soon savor.

CHAPTER

SEVEN

FELIX VERSUS FURBALL

The smell of fresh blood and guts. The mild burn of his muscles. The screams of fury and the dying.

And the salty taste of sweat mingled with splattered blood.

The gory reality of battle.

With Penny at Felix's side, the narrow streets and the tall stone buildings corralled the darklings toward their deaths. In the bright light of the lampposts, any moderately skilled Champion could make out the packs of lycan the moment they appeared.

The noise of their claws scratching the cobble. Their grunt and growls echoed and amplified. Their snarls and howls. All a clear warning another pack was coming.

And the stink of wolf and tiger drenching the still air.

Another obvious sign.

Most of the citizens had already rushed inside the buildings. Whether they belonged there or not. The generosity of strangers in dire times wasn't exactly uncommon in this land. The bangs and grating of heavy furniture shoved over to barricade the otherwise flimsy pine doors. Stacked against the shuttered windows on the first floor.

A good strategy to reduce casualties from a small darkling raid. A solid delay if this was a full invasion.

But the hordes of spidora that the vixen Snow slaughtered on the rooftops ...

Felix seriously doubted this was a mere raid. Penny and him had already swept down a few blocks. With stands overturned. Shattered. Scattering the fruity or meaty snacks everywhere. Wagons broken. The horses cut down. Dying when not dead.

And more than the occasional human too.

Especially in the darker areas between the bright lampposts. Where the wild lycan felt most comfortable. Most powerful. Most intimidating.

Savoring the quick deaths of their helpless human prey.

Not in itself unusual for a night raid. The wild lycan were as brutal toward humans as the human pelt farmers were to the lycan's domesticated brethren. The beasts' irrational hatred of mankind driving them to ugly feats. None caring the damage it eventually inflicted on their domesticated brethren.

So slicing their throats, breaking them like twigs, crushing them like roaches – Felix only wished he could wear a wild lycan's pelt as he did so. These beasts wiped out his entire village for no reason. His homely mother in her gray moo-moo and perfectly tart peach pies. Dead. His father in slacks brawn drenched in sweat from working his field of corn and cotton. Determined to earn enough to send his youngest son of a few years to an academy. Dead.

But ignorance of humanity was also the lycan's greatest weakness.

Having survived the lycan raid that destroy his village, retained his senses from a strict diligent upbringing, Felix gathered all the money and wealth from the ruins he could carry – the dead didn't need it. And the lycan didn't take it.

And it paid his way into the academy, into the life of a Paladin.

Paid for his family's, his village's revenge.

Many times over.

Screams came from the next block. Growls and snarls.

The taste of salt and blood clung to his mouth.

Felix tightened the grip on his saber. Its blade hexed to cut anything except the black leather sheaths that were magicked to hold it.

"Penny," he said, "Hurry."

And dashed down the winding street.

Ears perked for any other sounds. The taps of the girl's boots faded behind him.

Her speed not quite up to Champion levels.

Yet.

His eyes kept peeled for any misplaced shadow. Whether among the ruins in the street. Or as shadows against the sky. Distortions by the rooftops.

Nose sniffing for the stench of beast. Whether spider, lycan, or rat – or together.

Because it meant a full invasion.

A full invasion met ratlings. Giant brutal ratmen that made wild lycan seem gentle and civilized. Many wore black plate armor. Wielded huge wicked blades skillfully made. All highly trained in battle – many as formally as informally.

And none ever deterred by hatred to study their enemies.

A ratling likely led the invasion. A skilled general. One comparable, if not better, in intellect and power than most human generals.

More than one, maybe.

But crush the ratling leaders in front of their men …

The first lycan corpse popped into sight. A blue-grey tigress curled awkward on top of two humans. Blood pool underneath them. Congealing.

Civilians successfully killing a lycan warrior?

Unlikely.

He dashed over.

Spotted the first thing wrong. Her fur was far too silky. Her build – too soft, slim, and femininely curvy compared to its wild brethren. Even her black stripes seemed placed too carefully. A sexual intent rather than the usual more random natural way.

A domesticated lycan. Bred for the whorehouses. Escaped to a hidden lycan village – and then enslaved as a purren.

And a victim as much as those humans.

Felix clenched his teeth. Baring them unseen at those wild monsters responsible.

But kept running. The living needed saving. Not the dead. The dead could wait.

Forever if necessary.

When the tigress hacked out an explosive cough. Shuddered and twitched.

He jumped to a halt.

Turned.

Crept closer. Blade ready to end her suffering.

Because only the domesticated lycan deserved mercy. Unlike their wild brethren, they were mentally and emotionally somewhere between pet cats and dogs, loyal and friendly with the right upbringing, and genuine humans, with a human's intelligence and more.

The tigress even had a familiar exquisitely sexual built – ignoring the blue-grey fur and cat parts. Even her movements as she moaned, tried to pulled herself up, belied how thoroughly her line was bred for the whorehouses.

Likely she was one of the highest priced breeds for it.

Like poor Rose.

Now the Paladin nicknamed her Bloody Rose. Who still hid the fact she was in truth a red vixen escaped from a pelt farm – a new exotic breed meant for the whorehouses. Hid as a human redheaded urchin kid for years. Stealing not only for herself but for plenty of other worse-off orphans.

Till she grew old enough. Matured into a gorgeous beauty.

And ran away from that past.

Started anew as a songstress. Would of gone far.

Except her secret was discovered by the wrong person. That she was one of the few lycan who escaped the pelt farms, escaped the whorehouses, or escaped whatever enslaved horror they were forced to live under – and who hadn't fled the human world.

Because a street kid knew better than to assume those hidden lycan villages were any safer.

A hunch that was right.

And those street smarts were reason she located the Earth Wizard. Convinced him to support her, rescue her. To hid her lycan identity throughout her training and career.

Why she was sent safely to a distant land rather than stationed here.

Yet her blade and nose today would of saved many people. Locating the ratling generals would of been far simpler with her guiding him.

A monstrous screech broke his line of thought. Echoing everywhere. From all directions.

Joined by three other roars.

Then cut off.

Felix froze. Listened hard.

The sources – definitely some kind of incredible danger.

Screams of the dying drenched the air. Howls and snarls of mundane darklings. The crack and scratch of numerous claws against cobble and stone. The same stink of blood and guts.

Of the dead and dying.

But he had to find the newest danger. The greatest danger. The troops stationed in this city, given time, stood some chance to trimming down the darkling numbers, not the more extreme monsters.

Not just slow the ratlings hordes.

That was his job.

Felix, as the only Champion remaining in the land, was the only soldier capable of ending the threat no ordinary soldier could stop. His duty demanded it. The wizard already insisted he avoid the giant ratling's final challenge at Storm Killer.

No time for this tigress now –

"Hey, Paladin Guy," said a sultry kitty voice, "I'll tell you the invasion plan for the right price."

FELIX SNAPPED his attention toward the voice.

The blue-grey tigress sat comfortably, suggestively, on her heels, on top of the human bodies, as if they were merely a carpet on top of the bloody cobble. Her fur still crisp and clean against the humid heat drenched with the stench of battle.

Not a drop on it.

The rainbow painted wall close behind her clearly contrasted it too. The light from the lampposts here bright rather than dim. Bright enough to give her coat a gentle sheen.

As if she intended to be found by human soldiers. Try to seduce them. By the coin offered for her pelt if not more sexual ones.

A common ploy to ambush human troops.

Yet she held her palms up facing him in surrender. Trim claws out but clearly a third the size of wild lycan. Her breasts clearly larger than the typical beauty – tigress or human.

Those crisp blue eyes large yet closed just enough to look lazy on her round friendly face. Her small smile coming off smug.

Just like Rose's when she was nervous. It came with the breed.

He also kept his blade pointed at her.

Even Rose knew how to deceive a human that grew too trusting too soon, by pure instinct.

"Purren or free?" asked Felix. Listening for Penny to catch up.

But the tap of her boots – not a single sound.

"It's ... complicated," she said. Adding a cutesy cringe shrug.

"Are you oath-bound or not?" he asked.

"Technically no," she said, "But my three masters think so."

Felix could only raise his eyebrow at that. According to Rose, purren oaths went to one master only.

But she did have limited experience with her own kind.

"Three?" he asked, "And they know about each other?"

"Yes and no," she said, "Respectfully."

A quiet purr came from her too. Another sign of nervousness here. Not, as many naive people thought, happiness. Not always.

Not in this situation.

He fell silent. Resisted speaking immediately.

A domesticated tigress that dared risk tricking its wild brethren?

Azure Snow herself risked severe punishment disobeying whatever orders her master gave her in order to destroy that spidora hive. Risk saving humans rather than dying with them.

That fact that Felix could of slaughtered the darkling bugs by himself easily … it still spoke of her great bravery. So he gave her a coded message that Ash should understand no matter how drunk he got. A message her lousy tigress master would never catch until it was too late.

But would guarantee Snow freedom – and a future among the Paladins – if she wished it.

This tigress on the other hand … she could very easily be a trap. Seductive deception was bred in the whore breeds. All in order to better please the whorehouse's clientele. It was practically instinct. Poor Rose couldn't even help resorting to it no matter how often her friends called her on it.

One of the reasons her and Ash never went from romantically crazy drinking buddies to full-fledged relationship.

"What do you want in exchange?" he asked.

"Well," she said, tilting her head, "I'm quite the well-traveled girl. Name a city and I've been there. Smelled the sights. Heard the histories. Cuddled the riches. Borrowed a thing or two. Lots to see and do. Including here. Like see the Tavern of Vasery."

"Borrow a vase or two," Felix said. Each a priceless treasure that could somehow bottle and preserve liquors for countless centuries. Many currently filled with priceless wines from plants no one's seen in countless generations. Only the wizards themselves could identify them.

Only some of them.

"Exactly," she said, "Traveling is kinda expensive. And a

girl like me can't stay anywhere too long, take just any job. Can't risk anyone seeing my ears and tail and all. Lots of prejudice toward us kitties because of our nasty wild cousins."

The very implication forced Felix to steady his pounding heart.

It couldn't be.

Was this tigress the apparent solution to the most perplexing mystery and vast conspiracy of grand darkling thefts this age? One that befuddled and defied the active investigations of five whole teams of the best Paladins sleuthing away for the last four years without uncovering a single lead.

Felix couldn't help but laugh.

Then lowered his blade. Pointed it away from her.

Kept it ready if she lunged.

Couldn't be too careful.

"Tell me the plans," he said, "And I'll give you something better."

That perked up her ears. She definitely scented his honest intention.

"Better than the Vases of Honeyed Gold?" she asked.

The most valuable vases of the whole priceless collection? None were even stashed in the Earth Wizard's home. Let alone the Tavern.

Because the wizard hid them somewhere deep in the catacombs underground this city. Guarded by powerful magics and monsters. Some more ancient and powerful than the Earth Wizard himself, supposedly. All because each liquor granted a power too dangerous even for the best Champions to try.

Felix sighed.

A very healthy but dishonest ambition. Normally, he'd offer a different solution but one that nailed her underlying problem directly.

"Not quite," he said, "How about the first key to it instead?"

Nailing two serious problems in one ... it was a huge gamble.

A necessary gamble now.

Her slow blink. Deepening purr.

"I'm in," she said, "The key then the plan, okay?"

"Ash La Pushka," Felix said, "The wizard's only son."

"I see," she said. Lowered her hands below her shoulders. Palms still facing him.

Then curled her tail around her waist.

A scream louder than the rest. A human scream. Among all the other screams of battle.

The sound clawed his back. Demanded he return to the fight. Leave the tigress rather than waste any more time here. She clearly wasn't an outright enemy of humans. To her sort, mankind free and prosperous created too much wealth simply to exterminate. Not that she was a friend either. Just not an enemy.

No.

He locked his legs in place for a moment. Refused to leave.

"Some bloodline keylock thing. Good," she said. Her pose

remained relaxed despite the stenches around them. Despite his obvious urge to return to battle.

"So here's the invasion plan," she said, "The first stage is lycan and spidora raids. Then ... vandread."

"Vandread?" Felix said. Ice goosebumped his skin. An undead monster of incredible strength, speed, and agility. With one to three innate, deadly powers.

And the ability to regenerate from any damage.

An invincible foe that despised the living. Its only weakness a secret specific to each individual. A weakness that had to be kept somewhat close to its body. It's will bound to a living master. A master whose death didn't end the vandread's existence.

No.

It merely freed it.

One of the few enemies any sensible Champion feared to face. Bound or unbound.

A single vandread could easily massacre this entire city. Even if it needed to hunt down the few who escaped its clutches.

"The vandread," he said, "Tell me everything you know about it. Now. Before –"

Suddenly a strong whiff of cherry hit him. Slimed his skin in the direction he had been running toward.

"Don't worry," said a new sultry voice, "I'll tell you plenty – if you live long enough."

And something hard slammed into his back.

CHAPTER

EIGHT

PETRA THE SULTRY NEGOTIATOR

With the streets so cramped, the lampposts lit the stone wall up to the second of several too many floors. Lit up every brightly painted streak of wavy exotic fruit or twisty heart or other weird human fetish thingy. Windows shuttered as if the human's insides could shut out the invasion of crazed darklings.

Even with the blood splattered on the lower walls. Turning the lovely decorations gruesome. The stinky gore scattered on the streets. The corpses below her legs and elsewhere.

Petra could still smell the bitter fear of the humans crowding, trembling within the buildings.

Even if it took some effort. Had her blood been boiling hot like her wild cousins, she would of never noticed it.

Not with the screams of the dying in the distant echoing as loud as if her snarling wild cousins. Their howls and other racket from slaughtering humans could of come from the next block down.

Only the scents on the humid breeze warned her they were several blocks away.

Not that they would show her much more mercy than humans. Enslave her rather than kill her. Kill her like the two human gutted corpses under her legs. Their bodies already cooling down. The smell of death coming from them.

But the bodies protected her fur from the blood congealing on the rough cobble. The jagged stones were bad enough on her delicate foot paws. Sitting on these kinds of streets without any blanket was hard at the best of times.

Terrible anytime else.

Still, tricking three wolves into thinking she had purrened herself to them – her luck would only go so far. A blue-grey tigress was considered rare but desirable among her wild cousins. Thought of as lovely airheads who, whenever they tried to be clever, failed all the time.

So those wolves merely smirked. Their sardine sour scents suggesting they thought Petra had been tricked into purrening herself to those louts so clear.

And so wrong.

The giant dark-skinned Champion that had towered over her – with his square face and pulsing brawn – oddly smelled of sweet candy mercy and sympathy than only of blood and coppery bloodlust. His navy coat and slacks splattered with plenty of blood and gore too. None thick enough to cover completely cover the scents of his comrades – a drunk young women and an even more drunk young man.

His sword was covered with blood and gore too. From her wild cousins, from the stink of it. Rumor had those blades were sharp enough to cut anything except their sheaths.

A rumor she managed to test a few times by borrowing a blade or two. Nice for trimming hair, fur, and claws if you were careful enough.

But even Petra was too smart to hold onto them too long. No Paladins didn't exactly like when any non-Paladins held one of their precious blades.

The blades all still fetched good coin though.

But when the blond human girl descended from the sky. A peached color girl in red sultry straps waving their long ends in a wind that didn't exist. Flapping wings of serpentine backbone out of her back. Coiling and wavering. With a side of straight flexing, sharp ribs. That cherry and vanilla stink gnawed the nose. That white smirk ... worse than any lusty wolf.

A vandread as beautifully built as any tigress from the pelt farms. Even Petra herself. A tigress from a well-bred bloodline worth many, many coins for even a single kitten before she blossomed into her mature sex toy self.

And the overwhelming sense of dread weighed Petra down. Like iron chains chilled icy.

All Petra could say what it was "Vandread."

The Champion didn't catch the meaning. Despite her eyes glued to the most dangerous of undead creatures landing behind him. His brave heart must of deflected the vandread's inherit terrifying presence.

Not until a snake bone wing slammed into his back.

Flung him into a wall.

The crack sent hackles everywhere on her body on end.

The vandread even spoke. Yet Petra pounding heart drowned out her sensitive ears.

Petra merely held her hands up. Palm out. Small claws out but certainly not threatening.

Those puffy red lips of the vandread pouted at her.

But its blue eye seemed to smile. Enjoy a lowly tigress' suffering.

Enough for its snake wings to arch up.

Point right at Petra.

Sharp ends aimed right at the lone poor lycan.

Ready to spear her dead.

They shot forward.

Petra froze.

Heart stopping.

Knowing her scream would soon join those of the dying. The dead.

A scream that erupted from her lungs before they struck her.

"Wait!" screeched Petra, "I've got info! Lots of it!"

But the wings didn't stop.

Until the Champion smashed into their side. Knocking them aside. Mere feet from their fatal target.

Petra's coin-maker chest.

The tigress gasped. Panted. The pounding in her ears too loud, too quick to hear anything else.

The thick bloodlust in his scent, tempered by sweet candy compassion ... maybe Petra would offer him a little romance ...

if he wanted it. A protective lover with the right connections – not exactly a bad thing.

Especially if she had borrowed something whose prior owner now insisted she return sooner than never.

The Champion lunged at the vandread. Dodging another swing of her bone wings.

Loping it off midway.

The vandread's scowl ... enough to freeze Petra's blood over several times. Its wing already began to regenerate quickly. The old wing flopping violently on the cobble.

Wiggling loudly toward the Champion.

While he charged the last distance to the blond undead.

She leapt back. Losing an arm.

Giving her a moment to strike. Both wings spearing his back.

But missing.

Instead her midsection was sliced through. Her upper torso cocking awkwardly.

Then he cut her wings off.

Yet all regenerating quick. Yanking anything back together. Nothing falling off.

And the vandread grabbed his sword hand. Locked it in place midair. Above her head.

When those red strapped all arched toward the Champion.

About to stab his vitals everywhere.

And the very sight seemed to stab Petra's own vitals.

"Wait!" screamed Petra, "He knows Ash La Pushka! Kill him and –"

The vandread halted instantly.

Her eyes spearing Petra.

"Ash La Pushka?" the vandread said, "Here? Really? Lie and your worse than dead, cat."

"Yeah," said Petra, "He's the target, right? Then –"

But the vandread suddenly stabbed the Champion with her straps.

Just as he sucker-punched her jaw with an upper cut.

Cracking the undead's neck so bad it slammed against her back.

Then bounced back up unharmed.

And she flung the big brawny man up, far above Petra. A loud crack, splitters of wood flying everywhere, as Petra's only savior smashed through a shutter so violently no human could hope to survive.

Not even a wolf at full strength could make it. Not without so many broken and fractured bones, so much internal bleeding, that it would die soon afterwards.

Forget a tigress.

Even the legendary Ivy Reap.

Yet fiery acid burned through Petra's veins. Despite only a smug smile on her lips. Her body relaxing.

But the vandread merely chuckled.

Then huffed.

Her cherry vanilla scent so thick Petra could barely stop herself from gagging. It was enough to make the tigress never touch another cherry or vanilla drink again.

So matter how sweet or creamy.

"He's nearby," said Petra, "So better hurry. Before he runs off. Gets killed."

But the vandread merely narrowed her eyes. Strutting closer.

Her sensual gait, despite bare feet on jagged cobble, swayed her hips and chest too properly. As if it were bred solidly into her. Even more than Petra's own bloodline.

Yet not a hint of cat ears or tail on the girl.

Just bones wings arched toward Petra. Pointed tips aimed at her.

Drying the tigress' throat.

A taste of milk vodka ... a single lick even before she died horribly...

Double or death, as the highest stakes gamblers said at the Gin and Goblin.

Well, before they lost. Big time. Died a worse death than most. All to win a prize no one ever won yet.

"His scent – wow," said Petra, "I never smelled someone so drunk. I nearly passed out just smelling it secondhand off that Champion guy. No way that Ash guy is going to survive long. Not with my wild cousins going wild, killing every human they can slice their claws through."

A gasp. The vandread froze her strut.

"I see," she said. Her voice as icy as it was sultry.

"Then I better get to him first," she said, "But if I don't find him ... well, there are worse deaths than losing an unpayable bet at the Gin and Goblin."

That wicked smirk. The sharp reference.

Apparently, this vandread knew more of Petra's past than she let on.

"Duke BloodTalon," said the vandread, "He'll never forgets a debt unpaid. And pays better than any to find thieves like you, little cat. So if you lied ..."

The vandread chuckled. The screams of the dying only making it crisper.

But Petra huffed. Smirked.

"No worries," she said, "I never return stuff sooner than never."

Even if her insides were chilled solid with bitter fear.

Even as the vandread launched herself into the air.

Vanished into the dark sky.

Ash nearly tripped face down into the cobble at the next darkling they ran into.

No way among the stone buildings and cramped streets did he ever imagine seeing the sight before him again. No matter how much alcohol he downed before this ongoing disaster of a night – Dead Man's Run pure and gut roaring, mulled red wine strengthened by rum and mint ...

Or even the Final Chug.

The screams of distant victims too sharp for his dulled drunk senses to dismiss the sight as mere delusion.

He would never forget that sweet smell of cherry bathed in mild vanilla.

Even if it didn't fit within the stinks of blood and terror drenching the night. The dark shuttered windows of the buildings around him. The lampposts and moon were all bright enough to allow his drunk eyes to see the street clearly enough. Hear the gasps of the two lycan girls behind him, no longer pushing him onward.

To see Amber standing tall and proud. Hands on lush hips that jutting out to greet her unfaithful Ash.

And dressed as queen of the femme fatale darklings.

In an outfit that showed every inch of her six crisp peachy foot body, as she once called it so long ago, a body that put those supposed perfect goddesses to shame.

A strap of white translucent silk around those heavenly bulges from her chest. Hugging her like a single, loose bandage. Another silk strap crisscrossed around her hips and up her groin, the long ends hanging loose to the side like sheaths to deadly legendary blades. Two more around her heel and zigzagged up her shins. A final two around her forearms, with very long loose ends hanging easy.

Like tooth vines about to snap prey and drain it of blood.

Penny would try to kill Amber out of spite.

Because two bone wings came out of Amber's back. Not bird wings. Or dragon wings. Like a pair of spines but with only one side of ribs. Spines that flowed as elegantly as snakes. Ribs that curved and twisted as elegantly as the spines.

And thinned to razor sharp tips at the end.

Ash couldn't help but gulp. Her cherry taste even reached his mouth. Filled it like a sweet desert.

Despite it being completely closed.

Words escaped him completely.

Her skin as peachy crisp and unmarred as the day he last saw her, stolen by those vicious lycan, to be broken and enslaved. Her long blond hair still the same lush golden color.

Especially the long lush lock combed over the left side of her face. Framing her oval face. Giving her pouting cherry lips an extra haunty zip. Electric blue right eye, narrowed yet smiling, ready to zap Ash dead.

As if unaware of the horrors standing beside her.

Two, thirteen-foot bucks. Carnivorous, judging by their deformed mouths baring fangs. Waving antlers as jagged and sharp as a pile of bloody swords chopped to a bunch of razor shards. Their long straggly hair twisting and twisting as if searching for an unwitting victim to grab and strangle.

Even if every dark brown strand shined and smelled like a chocolate – the exact kind of grooming nonsense some nobles did with their pet mutts.

And their noses were as red as a cherry tart.

The quiet deep mew beside Ash – it came from Mandy. Definitely sounded as sharp as her claws.

Followed by another growl, from the girl behind him. The bestial undertone different than a wolf or a tigress, yet definitely of vicious lycan.

A very vicious lycan. Really to tear apart anything in its path vicious.

Her finger jabbed his back extra hard – one of the very same fingers that kept Ash running despite his legs wobbling refusal at times.

Now it let him sputter out his first words to Amber in years. Ever since his cowardly self failed to save her from the lycan so long ago. Back when he was a growing teen full of young pride and dreams instead of a young man full of alcohol and regrets.

"Amber ..." he said, "I ... sorry. I. It's *so* good to see you."

Her pout turned to a small sardonic smirk. Sardonic. That's the type of good, many-coin word he saved up for only when she was around.

"Captured by lycan," Amber said. Her voice as lyrical as any songbird. "Pity."

And cocked her head up a bit. Giving him that bitchy chin up, nose up, look normally only born nobles managed to perform to full effect.

A look she admitted, during the epic drinking contest after their fifth successful show together, was as much to chase away boring, weak-willed guys as to mess around with guys too arrogant to know better.

"Yeah, uhm," he said, regretting overindulging in alcohol tonight, again.

And probably not for the last time.

"Not quite yet," he said, "Mandy and I have ... a drinking contest first. Our fight, well, it's complicated. I take it you're a darkling now. A true femme fatale, right? Dressed snazzy, slinky, and sexy evil."

Her bucks lowered their heads and stomped the cobble. Their hooves cracked so hard against the road that he expected them to break it.

The road, he means.

She also lowered her chin back to normal. Without the sinister stomping to go with it too.

"And you're a bit of a hero yourself," she said, "Dressed so snazzy. That saber – long, sharp, yet beautifully made. Just like a brave Paladin should. Definitely fitting for a hero's role. Think you can end me with it?"

The mews and growls coming from my lycan companions demanded he try.

In the most literal way possible.

The screams and cries from a distance too.

"End you?" he asked, "Not what I had in mind. Anyway, that's too predictable. Don't tell me going darkling made you go all cliche too."

Her smirk lost the sardonic edge. Grew a bit too.

But kept the sweet tartness of a cherry tart.

"Of course not," she said, "A girl revived from the dead can't be all old news. I got to set three conditions for my revival. Eternally youthful healthy beauty, absolute artistic license, and a certain weakness that's ..."

Her smile turned to a perverted grin as she lowered her head sinisterly. Raised her hands palms up letting the long straps hang off her wrists. Puffed out her divinely endowed chest till the translucent fabric stretched enough to show coin-sized red spots for her nipples.

Then arched her wings high like an undead swan about to impose its dark will upon a lowly worm.

"Quite dramatic. And silly," she said, "But befitting my ambitious nature."

"It better be," he said playful yet serious. A lesson, one of the few he remembered from the Earth Wizard, popping into his head.

She had to be a vandread. Both living yet undead. With

the undead's hunger for the living. Their great strength, speed, and agility. Possibly some magical powers too.

But her soul dwelled inside her body too. Complete with the mind, temperament, and personality of her original living self.

Able to heal or regenerate her body quickly unless her weakness was found and exploited.

But she was enslaved to her creator's will.

Outside of three conditions she set upon creation – including the exact nature of her weakness, the one thing that could either kill her or, even more secret, the additional part to bind her to a new master – the magic that revived her also compelled her to serve and obey her current master loyally and faithfully.

Yet he couldn't help but smile at her conditions.

"Greedy as always," he said, roguish smile matching my teasing voice, "Bet you're aiming to be the sexiest, scariest vandread in history."

The glint in her eyes somehow cleared his head better than it'd been in hours. No weeks.

No years.

The warm air crisp. His eyes, his limbs, no longer sluggish or wobbly. Everything was clear in the amber ale light of the lampposts, the milky white of the full moon.

So he rested the palm of his sword hand on his saber's hilt.

His hand even found it on the first try.

"Hate to cut your ambition short," he said, "But one of the darklings here will tell me about everything she knows about this attack on Chemarin. The first one gets the best deal. Love it to be you, Ambie Bambie, but that offer includes your fawns. And they're starting to look a bit twitchy, if you know what I mean."

The giant bucks snorted. Heads lowering. Steam puffing out their mouths and noses.

Her hands returned to her hips so quick Amber slapped herself.

"Oh, Twitchy and Scratchy always look like that," said Amber.

Cocking her head slightly to the side. Her hips shifted even more to follow.

But the rest of her curved trying not to.

Including lips pouting almost into a cherry sweet kiss – one of her sexier S poses reserved for diva roles and smutty posters.

"They're way too eager to feast on your flesh," she said, "Me? I'll stick to your lycan pals. The whole living undead part means I gotta eat the living. Might as well eat the race that tortured and killed me. No hard feelings, Ashtray."

"None taken," he said.

Curled his fingers around his sword's hilt.

"As long as there's none when I beat you," he added.

"Beat me?" she asked, "You gotta find my weakness first. A little hint –"

Her arms swept up. Her hands out at shoulder height. Palms point up to the sky.

"If you survive long enough, that is," she said, "Gotta grab life's fruits when you get the chance, or else, you know, a second chance ain't ever guaranteed –" her hands clenched into fists – "a first chance isn't either."

AMBER SMILED that cherry vanilla smile as sweetly as her scent. Her arms up, body curved in a sensual S. The ends of those silk straps of hers starting to flutter from her hips and forearms.

Yet Ash didn't feel a single breeze in the warm night air.

Not a single sound rang out across the street.

Only the screams and cries of distant innocents running into merciless darklings.

Her giant buck already shifted sideways. Spreading their feet. Leaving no space between them, Amber, and the buildings for anyone to pass through except under their legs.

Under their twitching long fur.

Not that Ash or his temporary lycan allies could turn around and run. The alleyways between buildings were far too thin to escape quickly. Not to mention the spidora and its hatchlings.

Take too long here and they'd catch up.

When the chorus of moans erupted behind Amber, Ash did reconsider a tactical retreat. As his fake dad Denzel Cole called it.

Even if it meant risking another encounter with the spidora.

Since the moment Amber revealed her weakness and its nature, her powers would grow. Or at least gave a very good hint of it. Even if it was just the three living people here. It counted. She'd become as much as three times as strong. If the bucks counted, then five times as strong.

And she'd probably announce it with a confusing riddle.

In fact, Felix, during a rarest of rare moment of getting drunk and actually opening up instead of sulking, admitted he'd avoid facing a vandread face on if he could – despite defeating a vandread was the mark of any legendary champion.

Because a vandread was one of the few darklings that required both facing a nearly immortal being head on *and* defeating it with its specific weakness.

So that fact Ash was still alive, in front of Amber the Vandread, warmed his heart to no end.

Behind Amber, the few human corpses that once laid quietly in the street began to climb to their feet. Their bodies swaying to an unheard, slow, but steady rhythm. Their hands wringing out toward us. Their pale distorted faces twisted in unholy hunger. While the gashes that ended their lives closed and healed over.

Then they all lumbered toward him and his lycan ... whatever's.

A good eight or so animated corpses.

That then halted behind the bucks. Split into two groups of four. Marched underneath the giants. Lurching fast as if whipped to speed up.

Two glassy thunks came from Ash's right – the clanks of Mandy putting two bottles, mostly full, down on the cobble.

The buck lowered their heads to charge. Antlers racks of razors capable to shredding all three of us to shreds.

Yet his legs didn't wobble this time.

Not yet.

The fact Amber, with her right eye, jolted his spine with its electric blue gleam. That cherry vanilla grin too. Even her legendary lock of blond hair hiding the left side of her face. Hiding it all except for her mouth and bottom of her rosy cheek —

Ash drew his saber and saluted her. Pointing his blade's sharp tip right at her divinely endowed chest.

Careful not to stare too long at those nipple spots.

"Mere ghouls won't stop me," he said. Going for the cheesy to irk Amber up a bit.

Not that her ghouls slowed.

Even when they neared the front legs of her monster bucks.

But Ash knew her weakness would involve either her own body, those straps, or both.

A vandread had a few basic limitations regarded choices for a weakness. The body part or object involved always had to remain "on her person" in wizard speak — basically, something she kept with her nearly all the time.

Like her own body.

Or those straps of silk.

Even if the weakness itself could be anything from eating a certain food to getting cut in a certain place.

Knowing her it would be as zany as her outfit.

Maybe kinky too.

"Oh really?" Amber said. Arching her nectarine eyebrow again. "Nice of you to let me know."

Then flipped her hand back and forth once.

"Try this then," she said. Adding a pert jiggle of her chest and hips.

A move he would of teased her on.

But his gut suddenly got socked by an iron ram of utter terror. One that racked his cowardly body with shivers.

With sweat.

With chills.

All so fierce his mouth tasted more raw bitter fear that cup of olive extract Penny forced down his throat thinking it was an olive oil latte during her rare urge to try cooking for him.

The ghouls themselves grew paler. More steady on their feet. Their movements less jerking.

Even grinning like cats spying a cripple mouse. Slowing down enough to drench Ash in their presence.

Sending his heart right through the hard cobble ground.

CHAPTER

TEN

EARTH WIZARD, THE
DISTRESSED DISCOVERER

On the outside, the house looked just like any other house here in Chemiran. A squat stone building. Two stories high. Tucked tight between two neighbors like eggs in a cushioned crate.

But with the small gap of an alley smelling of wine as fresh and crisp as the warm night.

Even with all the windows shutters closed and dark. Spaced several feet apart to perfectly match the average haphazard spacing common in the typical residential homes. The roof slanted and tiled. The ridge extended a foot or so to match the average too.

Except there was no visible hole in the iron lock on the thick oak door.

No sound from inside either.

The screams of the poor people dying by the scores made

the bent back of the Earth Wizard cringe a bit too straight. How the darklings breached the hundred-foot wall of stone and iron surrounding the city was anyone's guess. The celebration tonight would have lowered the wariness of the guards too much.

It only took one foolish failure too many for a disaster to strike.

The smell of blood and death would soon reach here. His magic was more than enough to eradicate the army of darklings butchering the innocents throughout the entire city.

Yet the marrow of his bones tingled from a deeper, darker spell waiting to be cast.

Forcing him to wait. Confirm his fears first.

Or else he might doom everyone by trying to save them.

The young petite Paladin girl now returned behind him was still absolutely silent. Amazing how her leather boots were so quiet against the cobble. Even if she was probably annoyed at not confronting the darklings head on.

But her flat face and skin complexion, that of those ripe exquisite apricots from the deep southern regions, would have attracted too much attention if they went the usual routes through the city now.

His loose yellow robes with silvery lining matched the style of the usual old timer scholars that lived their retirement here. They also hid the extent of his centuries of wrinkles and thin boniness. His gray whiskers and long hair were just unkempt enough to prevent anyone from examining him too long.

"Connie," he asked, "Found any other doors?"

"None," she said, "Unless hidden by magic."

The last bit spoken as tartly as the little lime pudding pies she loved to sneak off and feast on during her weekly day off – a little secret of hers he discovered unintentionally during his regular outings through the city and friendly conversations with friends and stranger.

Many of whom he would now never get the opportunity to chat with again.

Which sunk his frown deeper.

Death came to everyone. Eventually.

No need to speed up the process.

But the tingle in his marrow definitely came from this house.

"I doubt it," he said, "Hidden by magic, I mean. Your skills of observation are superb."

An honest compliment. He knew better than to assume everyone knew their own strengths and weaknesses.

Or understood his intent whenever he misspoke.

He only paused a moment for a response from her. None came.

"Stay close behind me," said the Earth Wizard, "And remember my prior orders. It is of utmost importance."

"But ..." said Connie.

"Please, Connie," said the Earth Wizard. Cutting off any protest before she could reveal any hint of what he had ordered. "It is vital."

"Yes, sir," she said.

Her stiff voice betrays her unease. As the last wizard, he knew if he died, she might face a severe punishment – except the message parchment he had handed to her, complete with a disguise spell to hid it from the wrong eyes, would redeem her and her honor.

If only he could tell her everything safely.

Hopefully, this precaution and his others would prove unnecessary.

"Now let us begin," he said, "Stay within seven feet of me unless I order otherwise."

"As you command," said Connie.

Her footsteps, as quiet as they were, still were loud enough for him to hear over the growing screams of the dying innocents blocks away.

She positioned herself four feet behind him.

A moment later he headed straight to the front door.

Pushed his palm against it.

It resisted.

His bones tingle as if the marrow inside had turned to living slime.

The smell of the iron lock. Underneath the blood and death of tonight's horrid massacre, that bittersweet bite of bloodiron – iron forged with blood potions so potent a sensitive nose could smell the blood potion within the iron once close enough.

A black pentacle burned itself into existence on the lock. With five demonic skulls in each triangle and a pair of giant demonic skulls in the center.

All with glinting eyes.

Making his blood run colder than the frozen wastelands at the caps of this world.

The Seven Kings of Hell. Beings each as powerful, if not more so, as the Dark Lord himself.

And none willing to humor coexistence with any denizen on this world.

Darkling or lightling.

The forced peaceful stalemate between lightlings and darklings was already falling apart. Without the help of the other three wizards that imposed it, it was doomed. Thinking back, the wizard debated if merely letting the darklings and lightlings live as they wished – divided and hateful of each other – rather than encourage mutual peaceful habitation in various cities and towns ... it still would have required a subtle, gentle hand to work.

More subtle, more care than the aid the wizard provided in starting the breeding of lycan in pelt farms over many generations to transform them from mindless murderous beasts on two feet to their more modern humanized selves, wild or tamed.

And the help of more wizardry than his own.

This attack would spiral out of control. Lead to another War of Light and Darkness. Exactly what the Dark Lord and his Dreaded Ones wanted. Where the Dark Lord would rise again and rule as a tyrant. Insist on eliminating any lightling against becoming an utter slave, body and mind, to their supposed darkling betters – yet the darklings themselves not much better off than their poor lightling brethren.

But there was no hope of marshaling a truce to defend this world against the Demon Lords. Even if all the lightlings and darklings stood in unison against them.

As he feared, the Earth Wizard had no choice left.

He had to enter this place. Undo whatever spell was about to be cast.

For if it failed, the Dark Lord and his darkling hordes would be the least of their problem.

CHAPTER

ELEVEN

FELIX AWAKENS

The warm soft cushion supporting Felix from below didn't diminish the ache coursing through his entire body. A gentle lavender smell mixed with rosemary and thyme attempted to comfort him. With a light cotton cover over his body and a down pillow under his head, Felix decided only to breath slower and deeper for a few moments.

To savor the moment of awakening to a second-chance in life.

Gather information without his sight deceiving him.

The murmur of a human crowd came muted through what had to be solid walls. The occasional crack and echo revealed the walls to be some sort of stone. Lacking windows, judging from lack of outside noises mixing in. Not a scream, a mutt's yelp, or a horse's neigh.

No hawkers hawking their wares either.

With a savory whiff of chicken broth reaching him too.

Made his empty stomach growl. His last meal so long ago he couldn't remember it clearly. Maybe a minced meat pie or some other snack.

Maybe not.

And that was before he accounted for how long he was unconscious.

There was no question this place was underground. Likely an illegal den in normal times. A refuge in these darker times. For the soldiers of Cheramin, who probably frequented these places more often than they cared to admit, wouldn't forgive the crooks if they refused the townsfolk and then the city survived.

No one would forgive them.

The slight cotton tension over his body – Felix still wore his Paladin outfit of a navy coat, shirt, and slacks. His boots, though, no longer on his feet. Only socks.

Fresh from the dry feel of them.

The last thing he remembered – the vandread stabbing him with her red straps. Flinging him high into the air. Helpless as a ragdoll lump, he smashed through shutters built of solid oak. Cracking bone and bruising flesh.

Then recalled nothing.

"You okay, Paladin?" asked the gruff voice of a grown man. Full of concern too.

Felix opened his eyes. Beside the bed was the speaker. A giant bald guy built more like a portly brawny troll than a human. Even if his features clearly marked him as human.

His beady eyes clearly glinted with intelligence softened by compassion.

"Yeah," said Felix, "Thanks, sir. I've had better days. But better alive than dead."

The man chuckled. His crooked smile seemed genuine.

The small square room was made of solid stone bricks. Moisture seeping through the cracks.

Clearly, they were underground.

"Don't we all," he said, "Friends call me Grunts. After my trusty club. Kept the hoodlums from bothering the good honest folk. Well, until today. Cracking the heads of a few lycan only seemed to encourage the vile furballs."

Felix smiled back. Grunts clearly knew the impression he gave to others, despite his more educated speech and demeanor – unfitting of his ragged beige shirt and dark trousers.

Yet used it honestly.

"I'm Felix," Felix said. "Felix Stormbringer. I'm sorry I couldn't do more. The vandread ... once I recover, I'll seek her out again. Destroy her. No one else here can."

And sat up. His back aching even more as he did. The mattress groaning as loud as Felix wanted to himself.

"No need to rush too quickly," said Grunts. Even if he didn't move to stop Felix. No. Instead, he handed Felix a bowl of chicken broth. Complete with chopped noodles and a fresh pine spoon. A bowl large in Grunt's massive hands.

The growl of Felix's stomach forced him to take it. To wolf it down.

It even had just the right amount of salt in it.

Pepper too.

"Before you go," said Grunts, "Would tell me what

happened? What you know from the beginning? It seemed for some reason the lycan and other darklings are avoiding the buildings. I thought they were saving them for later. But when you crashed through those shutters, well – if the residents hadn't left carrying you through the nearest secret passage the moment they did ... a horde of lycan smashed through the buildings. Destroying it completely, according to the residents."

So the Earth Wizard had begun to move. The old man was cautious. Probably concerned over a trap before he tried anything too drastic.

The soup was only half finished, yet Felix already felt revitalized. Its savory warmth flowing through his veins.

Yet the door only a few feet away might as well been miles.

"A protective spell," said Felix, "Probably. The Earth Wizard would never let Cheramin fall so easily. Not against a full invasion. Just be thankful no spidora were among those lycan."

"Thank the gods," said Grunts, "He's a good man, that Earth Wizard. I spoke to the residents who saved you. They said some strange things about the vandread – that she resembled a young promising playwright actress named Amber. Personality and looks. And that you saved a tigress... who almost got you killed. But I suspect some misunderstandings."

"Misunderstandings ... true," Felix said. But refused to say more. Not now. Too risky. Few sympathized with lycan, domesticated or not. And the vandread – if she lived in this city while alive –

But Grunts only sighed.

The murmurs beyond the stone walls still echoed quietly enough to soften the sound.

"If you don't wish to speak of it, say no more," said Grunts, "But if the vandread is indeed Amber, I can tell you quite a bit about her. She used to be my apprentice. Last I heard she got herself captured by the lycan. Killed with the other humans when the packs decided that human slaves were too dangerous to keep. Rumor had it a beautiful blond human girl inspired all her fellow slaves to revolt. Using a crude but effective play. Since the lycan were too uneducated to recognize what a play was. If true ... not exactly the worst way to go. I only wish I knew the truth – and that last play she wrote."

"It's true," said Felix, "According to the Earth Wizard. But if this Amber is a vandread, she may no longer be free to side against the darklings that killed her. She'll slaughter us all without compassion or mercy."

Grunts sighed again. Slumping.

"For a second chance at life," he said, "She'd only insist on artistic license. That and eternal beauty, health, and youth. Here's what I know of her ... afterwards, if you're willing, would you let me know ..."

"Yes," said Felix, "That and more."

They both nodded.

Certain of what must be done next.

CHAPTER

TWELVE

ASH, THE CRAZY STUPID DRUNK, PART II

Ash don't know how long he stood there. Heart pounding frozen acid in his ears.

The street between the stone buildings suddenly seemed too narrow. Too small for the giant bucks taking up most of the space. Their giant sharp hooves planted on the cobble. Steaming breath coiling out of their mouths and snouts. Huge sharp antlers down and ready to charge. Waiting for the pale ghouls marching underneath them to clear way.

Amber grinned her wide cherry vanilla smirk.

Her scent, mingled with his utter bitter raw fear, now as bittersweet as the thought that he would at least die by her hands.

But the chocolate scent she definitely gave her monster deer warmed his blood a bit. The sight of her peachy body built finer than any bottle of wine in Chemarin. A sight he had only believed, deep down, he would never get to see again.

To see her divine plump chest fruit and lush sleek hips in tight translucent silk straps?

Definitely 100% Amber. In a sexy femme fatale super-monster role.

Especially after she just turned a bunch of ghouls – basically the lowest class of dread not much better than rotting lumbering zombies.

Except they can regenerate.

And obey orders somewhat coherently.

Far more like the dangerous undead beings called revenants. More powerful if raised skillfully enough.

No.

Thinking dreads capable carrying out their own plans. Like slowing down as they marched under the buck's long bodies and legs. Who then prevented Ash and his temporary lycan allies from attacking the dreads.

So they could further drench us their terrifying-inflicting presence.

Yet dreads served and obeyed their master, utterly, loyally. Their old selves were only partly intact. Just enough to aid them in their goals and missions.

Aid them in the total destruction of the living too.

Their very presence inflicted an innate, paralyzing fear on the living.

Except vandread's.

Being both living and undead turned that paralyzing fear into a mere annoying worry, supposedly. Her superior acting skills hid any innate worry. Even that electric blue right eye gleamed wicked and confident.

"Good one," Ash rasped. The words forced out of his jaw. The touch of chocolate in the air saving him.

Let him push his body into a crouch.

Even if it was harder than breaking a thick fresh oak branch.

"But not good enough," he said.

Lifting his foot was like lifting a boulder., lifting an anchor that dragged it slower and slower.

Planting it down was louder than Penny's worst stomping temper tantrums.

Then he jerked his elbow down.

Cracking his blade up. Pointed toward Amber.

Then threw her another roguish smile.

Because finding Amber alive, even as a vandread darkling, was better than Ash had hoped. Enough to warm his blood a bit. That sexy outfit, so unpractical yet so theatrical, definitely was all her. Snake bone wings too.

"Not bad for a femme fatale darkling, Ambie Bambie," he said, "You've got the evil look and the evil nature down pat. Style too. I love how you don't overdo the ugly stuff. Monster bucks as ugly as a hog's dirty rear. Dreads as creepy as a peeping tom school. All I've got are two lousy lycan too scared to throw an insult, let alone a slash."

The renewed mew and growl of the lycan behind Ash definitely weren't entirely directed at Amber anymore. The cricks of their paw feet against the cobble probably came from their crouching even deeper.

Yet a practical vandread would of slaughtered his wisecracking ass long before he opened his mouth.

Well, actually, as soon as she confirmed his identity.

Probably.

But Amber?

She let out a wicked cackle. Hefty enough to jiggle her goods too. The echo snapped throughout the cramped stone street.

Warming his heart with prickles.

So what if he did end up dying here? His true love lived a happy life once more. Evil or not, a second life was still a life. She didn't exactly have a choice in the matter either. A vandread only got so much room to negotiate their three conditions too. Necromancy, as the Earth Wizard called it, wasn't always exactly fair toward the dead trapped in its spells.

But her conditions, though, let her live and serve her clustershit of a master happily as her dramatical nutty self.

Not some mindless bloodthirsty brute.

Since, well, just because her monster bucks were snorting and snarling at him, they did smell amazingly like sweet tasty chocolate.

Not that rotten decaying stink most evil things went with.

Far better than most darklings. They probably had stinking contests rather than drinking contests.

"Poor Ashtray," she said, "Afraid I can't help you this time. Be a man and save yourself."

Then pursed her lips for a long-distance cherry tart kiss.

"I'm *sure* you can do it," she added, "But those lycan –"

Bolts of blue lightning flew past Ash from behind. Missing his arms by mere inches.

And struck both monster bucks.

Engulfing each of them in a net of forking blue electric.

Their screams cracked the air. Their hooves smashed the ground.

Shook and jerked their massive bodies. Snapped their long legs. Their fur raging and whipping about.

Yet the electric nets held them.

Charging the air with the same bitterness of sparks that two blades smashing together sometimes made.

But far stronger.

Yet not as strong as the buck's fur suddenly snatching the dreads underneath the giant undead beasts.

The dreads tried to dart. To escape.

The fur was faster.

Wrapping around their undead, struggling bodies. Cracking their bones and skin. Sliding through their flesh despite it trying to regenerate from the damage.

Their screeches ignored.

Dragging them through the electric net. Even if it sliced through their bodies.

Sucking them into a raging ocean of fur.

The crunches and scrapping echoing sharp. Right through the narrow roads as the screams of the bucks.

Yet Amber merely arched her nectarine eyebrow in surprise. Her right eye sharper than before.

And focused on the lycan behind me.

"Snow now!" shouted Mandy.

Yet barely loud enough to hear over the screams of monstrous deer.

The electric nets suddenly vanished. Only the bitter stink of sparks left behind.

And the furious bucks pounded the cobble. Antlers down. Snorts full of steam.

Their eyes spearing the lycan.

"Hey, dinner steaks!" shouted Mandy.

Then chucked a tall angular glass bottle of clear bubbling liquid right at each buck's forehead.

Flying right across their eyes like a blindfold. Smashing apart. Splashing their eyes thoroughly with the contents.

Their screams made their prior screams sound like whispers.

His back suddenly had a familiar squirming feel. Because those bottles looked disturbingly like the vodka called Dying Man's Run – a vodka a bit less potent than Dead Man's Run.

Especially the bubbling clear liquid part.

And the bucks were now convulsing on their hooves too.

No.

He drank Dying Man's Run more often than Dead Man's Run to reduce the intensity of his hangovers the next day. No way something he put inside himself on a regular basis could cripple a pair giant wyrming undead monsters.

The next bolts of blue lightning ripped through the bucks. Quickly shredding them into little piles of ash scattered across the cobble.

Amber's smug smile no longer showed her vanillas.

"I ACTUALLY DRANK that stuff last time I was alive," Amber said. Her snake bone wings sinking to the ground. Flat and sloppy.

Her tone somewhere between amused and annoyed at herself.

As if her failed chocolate-smelling monstrosities never existed. The piles of ashes scattered across the cobble as worthless as that deaf singer long ago who had no talent and no will to improve.

Let alone improvise.

Forget the dreads and their short cannon folder roles. On stage – whether on the nice hardwood platforms in vast room of rows of raised pine chairs or the crude plank platforms built the same day as the performance in a park – those dreads would of been forgotten quickly.

Talent took risks, as Amber loved to say.

Well, before she was a vandread.

Hopefully now too.

Her eye looked right at Ash. But not at him.

Passed him.

"You were always quicker than me," he said, "I'm still at denial. That stuff wasn't Dying Man's ..."

But those loose straps hanging off her waist and wrists ... they seemed frozen in a wind that never existed.

Till the waist ones shot at him.

Passed him. One on each side.

Stretching but not thinning.

Gasps then chokes.

Fabric scrapping against fur.

Tightening.

Then an explosion.

The heat searing his back with icy dry chills.

The red sultry straps jerked back to Amber. Her pouty lips hooked in a gawk.

Apparently, this was one explosion she didn't cause.

"So you're the one hunting down the wizards," Snow said.

But her voice was far more confident. More lyrical too.

"And pinning it on your dead sister," Amber said, "Don't leave that part out."

"You clawing bitch!" exclaimed Snow. "The Fire Wizard wanted to teach her magic! He even bought her freedom!"

"Boo hoo," Amber said, "No one bought me freedom from you lycan. Well, besides the grim reap. But he's not exactly the one you want buying it. Even if he's a decent guy and all. Just saying."

"Mandy!" Snow exclaimed, "That's enough proof, right? Free me so I can –"

"No Snow," hissed Mandy, "I only promised to help you clear your name. Not to free you the instant I did."

"But ..." began Snow. Her tone clearly recognizing the futility of the argument before she began it.

So Ash broke in.

Because if the Fire Wizard was anything like his dad, the Earth Wizard, then Scarlet was probably not such a bad lycan after all. Snow neither.

And maybe not Mandy.

Too much.

In fact, sparing his life the moment he sputtered out the surname La Pushka, well ... not many human attackers would even humor this kind of nonsense. Forgot most darklings like spidora and ratlings and worse.

Not that he wouldn't win this contest. No question about that.

But when enforced by magic for life, unconditional servitude had one advantage.

The right order should basically be able to neutralize it. Give her real freedom.

Even if technically, her oath still bound her,

"Wait," he said. Too conscience that both lycan still stood close behind him. To his sides. "Mandy, Snow's your friend, right? Don't tell me your holding her because of our purren challenge. Let her go and ... um ..."

"No, Ash," said Mandy, "A purren oath is still an oath. I expect –"

"Hey, you idiots," said Amber. Waving her regenerated red straps around. "Powerful bloodthirsty undead darkling here. Remember? Ash for all times sake, I'll cut the chase because you're too dense to ever see it. Mandy's got tail twitch for you. Snow too, I bet, since lycan ladies prefer to date guys many to one. So –"

"Wait," Ash said, "What?"

The several feet of empty cobble between him and Amber seemed far more vast than before.

"Hey!" shouted Mandy, "It's just not honorable to kill a

purren challenger, even when the challenge is as stupid as a drinking contest, unless the rules –"

"Oh, shut it, catgirl," said Amber, "You like him or else you'd of sliced his throat long before he pulled the purren card on you. And with Snow and her magic –"

"I would never cheat a purren challenger," said Snow, "We lycan do have honor. Even if most of us are bloodthirsty idiots. And we're not much better when drunk."

"Then show me some of that bloodlust," said Amber.

Her sultry red straps now paired with arms to hips.

Then attacked the lycan.

The four red straps speared toward his sides.

Toward Mandy and Snow.

The several feet of cobble between Amber and Ash far too small now. The lampposts not bright enough. The stone walls looming too high. Their paintings too dull, as if their fruity colors were drained dry of their sweet cheerful touch.

Amber's straps stretching wiz, their near silent breeze, punched the night.

The now suddenly silent night.

The smell of roasted cherries and vanilla hit him. Her beloved scent. Far stronger than usual, of course, since a girl like her knew to wear it more subtly. But the whole undead thing, better safe than stinky.

And stark reminder what fate Amber might suffer if she lost to Snow.

Enough to make Ash glance down. Search for any other bottles of liquor. Pray that Mandy took more than two from the caffe. Especially since she to put some down before, it sounded like, at least.

And he did find two bottles.

Both knocked down, but both laid near him. One tall glass of bubbling clear liquid was a few inches from his heel. Another Dying Man's Run. The second bottle, a tall pitch maroon bottle with an extra narrow waist in the middle – right next to his toes.

Inside that bottle was it. That special red wine spiced with the mintiest of mints.

The Red Organism.

Its very existence spiked his heart with that warm bite that only the best red wines could manage.

But a giant burst of deep blue and violet flames roared from his other side.

Yanked his attention back to Amber. Her gleeful grimace glinted from the flames. Flames that heated his side as much as the lustful memories best not remembered right now.

From Snow's electric whatever added plenty of crackles.

Rips and tears from Mandy's claws.

Yet no straps attacked Ash.

Yet.

Now a normal hero like Felix the War God would announce a brave speech about how far his dear Amber had fallen to such deplorable depths. That he would free her from this terrible existence even if it cost him his life.

But Ash wasn't normal.

And *definitely* not a hero.

Especially since she got the jump on the obligatory speech before the final fight too.

"Now it's time to show me what you learned while I was away in heaven," Amber said.

Then cocked her head to the side. Jutted those lush hips out. Elbows in. Palms up.

Wiggling her fingers up at the sky.

"Okay, okay, it was hell," she said.

Licked her cherry lips nice and slow. As if tasting their juicy sweetness and savoring it.

"But hell's more fun," she said, "Really. Scary but fun."

Part of Ash actually wanted to ask, "Really? Hell?"

It wasn't like she was a good-hearted virtuous lass led astray in her last life. Her stuck-up bitchy persona did have a real-life component to it. Including being nasty, sadistic, and all together unpleasant when the time called for it ... and sometimes when it didn't.

But so what?

She was more honest than most people he knew. Less bloodthirsty too. Even as her current vandread state proved. Since other vandread would of wiped all of them out and reduced them to a bloody stain long ago.

So what if everyone back then said her some of her bloodier plays indicted a sick, twisted mind? Better a play with fake bloodshed than the real stuff. How many of those same people hesitated when it came to public stoning criminals, no stopping despite pleas of mercy, screams of agony from broken bones and gashes? When it came to pounding out their frustrations on those sentenced to the stocks for a bit?

Two activities Amber only watched on occasional, never actually participated in, tossing a play or two out there to try to gain sympathy for the ones convicted of sillier, harmless crimes like starving artists selling pornography to feed his family or some convicted as accomplices to coordinated thieving for merely feeding urchins some handouts out of sympathy.

The very same anti-heroes that few audiences sympathized with and often ended up jeering against anyway.

So they were very definitely wrong.

"Sounds great," Ash said, "Any pointers when I get there?"

Because if Amber ended up in hell, no way he wasn't either.

These two lycan too. How much innocent blood did they shed? No way they stood a chance, if Amber didn't.

Though judging from the sounds of their battle, they stood a better chance of doing well.

But yeah. As if he stood a chance against Amber's sexy straps of doom. Magical lycan lightning barely held its own.

Anyway, darklings had to go to hell, didn't they?

Useful info here, furballs.

"Sure," said Amber, "Try not to mess up too badly when you get there. It's a demon eat demon world. And word to the wise, avoid becoming a demon's pet. It's a lot like being a wyrm buddy ... but only the demon gets privileges – including ordering your cute ass around whenever it wants."

"Ouch, I'll remember that one," he said, "Anything else?"

Well, besides the glares from the lycan spearing his back. Because fighting a deathmatch usually involved, you know, actually fighting. Wars and raids too. In fact, combat in general, With swords and fists and arrows and so on. Kill or be killed, or severely wounded, or captured, and so on.

But Amber and Ash liked to do things differently.

Funner that way.

Of course, there's no way he could explain to these lycan's uncultured minds the intricacies of this normal, unpractical, but common theatrical technique against an overwhelming powerful enemy that he was using against Amber.

Especially the point that she knows exactly what he was doing too.

Or thought so.

"Yup," said Amber.

Perked out her plump chest fruit. Just to lure his wandering eyes back at her.

"Pretty talk goes pretty far down there," she said, "Smooth talking too. Just be sure to back it up when push comes to stab."

"No wonder you got yourself a second life *and* a sexier body under such good terms," he said, "I bow to the master of –"

"Hey!" shouted Amber. Wrinkling her cutesy nose. "No calling me master. My master will punish me – no, torture me, if I cross that line. Understand?"

"Oops," he said.

Bowing his head to his waist anyway.

Then glanced sideways unseen to look for the two bottles Mandy had put down.

"Sorry there, m'lady," he said.

Hearing that groan under her huff ... he didn't need to see her frown to know he was pushing a bit too far.

Better do this quick.

So he snatched the bottles. Both with his free hand. The minty red wine dubbed the Red Organism and the bubbly clear liquor aptly named Dying Man's Run up.

A skill perfected through much practice.

"Don't want to ruin your life – second life," he said, "A toast to your wonderful second life. Because what's the point of a second life if you don't have fun with it? Then we can get down to business ... eventually."

Her wicked smirk melted into a cheerful smile. Her eye sparkling with an electric more powerful that the magical lycan's ... electric frigid bolt attack thingy.

The crackles of lightning even fiercer. Mandy mews louder too. With her rips and shreds.

He had a feeling Mandy was really regretting accepting a purren challenge from him.

But Amber simply flicked the right side of her hair. Then slid her fingers gracefully down to her ear.

"You always knew the right thing to say," she said, "Sometimes."

He couldn't help but blink at the strange confession. Very out of role too.

"Okay," she said, rolling her eye, "Rarely. But better than never."

"To better than never!" he said.

Popped the bottles' corks with his saber's hilt.

Amber sighed. Closing her eye and shaking her lowered head.

How she could maintain a full sultry strap assault on two lycan, one very magical, yet barely pay attention – okay, seemingly not pay attention at all – no way any of the living here stood a real chance if she decided to get serious about killing any of them.

Mandy and Snow would only delay the inevitable.

Unless this plan worked.

So he walked the most dangerous few steps of his life.

CHAPTER

THIRTEEN

THAT FUCKING CAT

The never-ending tunnel of grey stone bricks, ancient skulls embedded throughout the cracks, and a musty smell that only the oldest libraries dared try aim for and missed entirely …

Petra finally managed to make out the dim glow of a rectangular doorway in the distance. The winding maze underneath Cheramin was bad enough. Avoiding the chattering humans huddled within some of the upper chambers was hard. They even sealed off several passageways ignorant of the depths of the maze.

But they definitely hadn't bothered to go down a level.

So many skulls gazed unblinking everywhere with glowing blue eye orbs. The kind of sight that made anyone's mouth dry more sour, more ragged than those powdered balls made of spoiled milk – that was the last time she ever crammed those cuties into her mouth for a desperate last-minute meal.

A meal gone horribly wrong.

The floor was smooth enough. Frigid but smooth. Like polished granite or marble.

But the same grey color as the walls.

Except for the occasional wide crack. She avoided those carefully. The edges look too sharp to risk even testing them. Not without a dummy to use on it first.

The amber glow of the rectangular door signaled the first half of her long journey was nearly over. As she walked closer, eyes peeled for any secret triggers – a hidden step revealed only by a slight cut in the floor that would sink upon touch and trigger a trap. Or a thread hung across the passageway that the unwary traveler would break by walking through and trigger a trap.

Or, more likely, simply cut off whatever limb tried to walk through it.

The cool air seeped through her fur far too well. The dampness already made her want to shudder. Maybe dry herself off with the silk towel she left back at the inn she had holed herself up in.

Well, had.

At least the darkling invasion of Chemarin worked as a great distraction. That Champion hulk's info hopefully will prove right after all. That that Ashy guy or his lycan body-guards never noticed her sneak up on them, syringe some blood out him quick, before they could figure out what happened ...

Then a quick jinx to make them forget what caused their surprise stop.

Losing the spidora chasing them, especially after those annoying spiders decided to go after her instead, for some bug-addled reason ...

Thank the darkness she knew a couple tricks to lose them.

All for the little glass vial of blood, she now held securely in her hand – but uncapped and scenting the air coppery. It held fresh blood from the very drunk, very male, very un-Paladin ally of the Champion.

Hopefully, Ash La Pushka's blood.

But now the humans in hiding were extra cautious about secret lycan. Eager to kill or chain any they caught. Wild or domesticated. It didn't make a different to them. Even if they could only hope to chain the domestic kitties like her, with all that breeding getting in the way.

It wasn't like she could point out how a Champion Paladin saved her then died fighting a vandread.

So when Petra reached the rectangular door, Petra only paused a moment to reach the various weird symbols. Guessing the ridge in the middle, with a tiny funnel wedged above the tiny channel, was where she was to pour the key.

Her heart thunked too hard now.

A dupe to do this for her ... much safer. Sometimes these doors were traps themselves. Scholars who could read these weird symbols could at least get a hint at potential dangers and all that.

But you never got rich but playing it safe.

Well, unless you were already rich and comfy.

So Petra poured the blood into the funnel. It flowed down the channel. Into the frame.

A crack erupted. The door shifted out from its frame.

Then its glow faded.

Then slid inward. Tilting out to one side.

Forcing her to jump back.

Yet only a pitch blackness remained in the doorway. Not even the glow of the skulls' eyes could penetrate it.

"Free!" cried some guy with a cutesy voice, "I'm free! At last! Freedom, here I –"

Something smacked into her chest.

Petra caught the thing by instinct. Her nose, hands, and fur told her the rest.

It was a kitten. A tabby kitten. With black bat wings. And an orange scorpion tail.

Moaning perverted now.

"Get back here, you damn pervert!" screamed a voice Petra hadn't heard in years, "Or else I'll skin you alive and all your damn copies!"

Instinct born from much experience kicked in and Petra jumped back a bit more.

Just in time for the redheaded vixen of her childhood to leapt out of the blackness.

"Rose?" asked Petra.

The green-eyed vixen blinked. Her red fox ears perking up. Those plump red lip dropping. Framing a peachy face with lush ruby hair down even more to her left side.

Yet she wore the outfit of a Paladin. Tight and tailored to show every one of her slim sensual curves.

Matching that gentle strawberry scent that humans could only smell when right next to her.

But other lycan could smell from further.

"Petra ..." said Rose, "I ... you came right in time. My days as a Paladin ... even with Felix and Ash to back me up – a lycan's a lycan, as they say. And I'm not about to be sold to some whorehouse. You with me?"

"Always," said Petra. Catching a very weak whiff of ancient wrinkled old fart, similar to that Earth Wizard that sneaked around the city, but different. "So the winged cat ... our first catch?"

"Leo the Magnificent is not a catch!" cried out the winged cat. Raising its front paw up high in defiance.

Despite its perverted face still drooling between her boobs.

"Wait, wait," said Rose, "Aren't you Leo the Great? Or was it Leo the Grand?"

"Don't go confusing us," Leo said, "We created mind-links for that. Can't have Leo the Great and Leo the Grand losing track of who's who. Or those two thinking they're Leo the Grand and me thinking I'm Leo the Great. Too confusing."

Rose grimaced as sardonic as any cubling forced to stuff a raw peeled lemon in her mouth.

"Yeah," she said, "Exactly. So now that you helped created that vandread to –"

"No, no," said Leo, "My latest ultimate creation! Gives me tail-twist just thinking of her. Tricky to make too. Duplicating a ... wait! Ha! No tricking me! A poor little destitute manti-core ... after I helped you killed these other wiz– AHHH!"

Petra pricked the kitten's ears with her claws.

Then meeting each other's eyes, Petra raised the hackles on her back for herself and Rose. No wonder no one ever found a hint of that infamous lycan witch Scarlet Knight. An inside job, Petra almost purred a laugh, must of netted Rose a good bounty from whoever enlisted her. Assuming they didn't decide silencing her afterwards was necessary. A tendency too many darkling higher ups followed. Forcing creative escapes and establishing new, secret identities after the best jobs.

So killing this winged kitty down here in secrecy of the vast underground ...

But slid down that road and she'd end up no better than her wild cousins. A job was a job. Go beyond that and might as well gut squirrels and gnaw on their gamey little bones. Start learning to live in dinky little tents and other primitive dumb stuff.

Even Rose realized it.

Helped Petra realize it too.

The same common sense saved them from the usual enslaved fate of other escaped lycan. From running to their wild cousins and getting their cute little butts enslaved.

"I'm sure the vandread let you enjoy her goods too, one day," said Rose, "As long as you –"

"Sorry," Leo said, "But your debts not paid. Not her original's either. Nobody's actually. The Vase of Honeyed Gold will only cover some of it. Of course, I'll permit your gals to retain a few samples. But first, you both need to prepare properly. A few missions beforehand should do. And cover your debts too. So everyone ends up happy. Right? Right!"

Rose clearly forced a sigh. Petra could only grimace in sympathy.

"Fine," said Rose, "I'll bear you-know-who a litter and give them to you ... but if you mistreat my cubs ..."

Petra gasped. Ice chilling her insides. Colder than any stone underground.

But Leo laughed.

"No worries," said Leo, "Your sisters each agreed. And I promised to take good care of them. The experiments won't hurt them a bit. Not much at all. Anyway, it's the only way to save your race from–"

"Leo!" shouted Rose.

"Okay, okay," said Leo, "But if you want Petra to be any help, to get a good deal, she'll need to know the whole story ... right?"

"Right," said Petra. Purring a bit louder. Saving her race from whatever, as a member of her race, definitely worth her time.

Was it a curse? A certain ancient artifact, the Vase of Honeyed Ruby, could lift any curse. Hidden deep below in these very passages guarded by monsters and traps unknown. The rumors backed by some secretive notes she borrowed from the soon-to-be-deceased Earth Wizard.

Something this Leo had to know. Something that suggested Leo had other reasons for this nonsensical breeding idiocy.

So that when the time came, Petra could strangle this batty kitten herself.

But for now, she merely scratched its ears and let the pervert giggle and drool over her chest fur.

Rose's slight smile.

Nod.

They'd strangle this Leo together.

When the right time came.

FOURTEEN

ASH AND THE CRITICAL MOMENT

The moment of relative silence pricked every inch of Ash.

It was actually quiet outside the booms and rips of battle coming from the lycan. No screams or cries in the distance. No carts over cobble or cacophony of crowds or taverns. Not even an echo from the random bang or crack.

Cities like Chemarin were never so quiet. It was disturbing enough to make his gut uneasy.

With the electric lycan bolts tearing through the air, ripping up straps, stinking the now chilly air like it was full of sparks from smacking swords – with the cherries and vanilla scent going from sweet to roasted sweet – from the mews and growls behind him turning to snarls and yowls ...

Every step seemed a mile. The uneven cobble jabbing through his boots. His outfit weakly attempting to hold him back. The two bottles in his hands, uncapped, slushed their potent alcohol loudly, their scent nipping him sober, his wobbly legs steady.

The lampposts already dimmed as it trumpeting his inevitable failure and death. The looming stone walls of the buildings a tomb. The once bright painting decorating them splattered with blood. Darkened, grim. Heavy as the dark above.

As if each and every twinkling star was glaring at him. The giant white moon like an eye spearing him with as much scorn as his fellow Paladins. As dismissive as Amber's single electric blue eye often was toward those without a true sense of humor.

Because Amber was always that free spirit type. Willing to risk life and limb over what her loved rather than what everyone said she was supposed to. Even when others insisted her loves were insane and stupid.

So he finished walking over quietly. Letting the bottles slush a little extra loud at the last step. Made the bubbles in Dying Man's Run pop a bit louder. It's wasn't like he intended to sneak up on her.

Not that his Paladin training wouldn't of helped him.

The moment she looked up he was right in front of her. A couple feet apart only. The closest he'd been to her for so many years. His old gorgeous peach of a dream. His dear beautiful Amber smiling at the chance for one last chug and hug together.

Even if, with him, she always hugged fully clothed.

Those sultry strap of doom were still plenty busy with those lycan not to interfere.

Lifting both bottles up, close, between their faces, Ash said, "I call Dying Man's Run. Poetic whatever, you know."

"Irony, you mean," she said, snatching his favorite wine of wines, the Red Organism.

Raised it.

"Cheers to my amazingly awesome new life of evil," she said, "Or your rather pathetic life of boring Paladin stuff."

Only if one of us died again. Tonight.

So he raised his Dying Man's Run. Savored her cherry vanilla scent one last time.

And said, "Boring's almost as bad as dead. Cheers!"

They clicked bottles.

Above the sound of battle, it rang out louder than it should of.

But didn't echo like it should of either.

Still, so what? They swung their bottles up above their lips.

She chugged deep. Would finish in moments.

Normally, he'd finish a couple moments after her. Losing the match, symbolically, at least.

Except he tossed his high into the air.

Stepped back.

Swung his saber up. Slicing through the strap around her plump chest fruit. Right in between her boobs.

Snatched the silk with his free hand. Shoved in his trouser pocket.

It snapped, not resisting a bit.

His eyes jerked to her throat. His cheeks flaming at his whole face.

Especially at the very thought of the next step.

A very desperate gamble.

Yet she hadn't even stopped chugging the wine bottle. An actress to the end. Those plump chest fruits were ripper and peachier than any sweet here, heaven, or hell. Those cherry coin sized nipples worthy of a king's treasury.

Gotta grab life's fruit with labor, right?

So Ash grabbed her right boob with his free hand.

As soft, silky, and warm as he ever imagined it. The nipple pointing his palm a nice perk.

Then pressed his forearm into her left boob. Over her nipple in all its warm, soft, yet pointy nature. Poking through his coat even.

Yet she didn't commit the expected gasp and spew of alcohol. Then the required scolding glare and inevitable slap afterwards. Harsh and rightfully deserved. Insults throw. Worded to rip at his very soul ...

Amber merely continued gulping down the wine.

Hell or undead, she didn't let anyone change her priorities.

His heart pounded so hard, blood flushed so hot and sweet, her cherry scent might as well have been coursing through his own veins.

The moment she tossed the empty bottle, he spotted the glint of fear in her blue eye. A sad smile on her lips.

Her cheeks more blushed than usual after a chug too.

Very understandably right now.

"Well, Mister Hero," she said, gently, "You got me. Congrats. Make it quick – alright? I –"

Then he kissed those cherry lips with every ounce of love and yearning stored in him since the lycan tore her away.

CHAPTER

FIFTEEN

THE EARTH WIZARD,
DISTRAUGHT DISCOVERER

Mustier than a thousand-year volume full of dust, mold, and cobwebs. Squeezed into a thick rectangle of cracked plaster and splintered rotting pine. The floor warped beyond recognition.

Enough to make the Earth Wizard gulp down the bitter bile from his dinner of sautéed steak tips and mushrooms.

The darkness shrouding the hallway so thick beyond a few feet that not even a spidora's beady eyes could hope to penetrate it. The taste compared to the humid air outside. Dank. Cool. With the aftertaste of iron and rotten lemons.

An aftertaste of incredibly dangerous dark magic.

The same magic that already suppressed the screams of the dying from outside. Despite being only blocks away, the stone walls of this squat house shouldn't be able to mute the sounds so well. In fact, they should cause more echoes and amplify them in unsettling ways.

His magic sight already limited to seven feet.

And the range of his powers.

Yet the decaying walls also acted as blocks against his power.

Thankfully, he detected that Connie already stationed herself three feet behind him. Sword drawn.

Not showing any impatience as he stood in the doorway of the mysterious house.

Peering closer at the decaying walls, squinting so hard every wrinkle on his face hurt, then the inside of his forehead – but he finally spotted the flickers of absolute pitch-black oozing like oily molasses within the cracks.

"Don't touch the walls," the Earth Wizard said, looking up toward the ceiling, "Touch nothing unless I – dear Godhood in Light!"

The ceiling ... once moldy plaster cratered and cracked nearly beyond recognition, now barely holding back an ocean of the oily pitch-black darkness. Some already seeping throw. On the verge of dripping yet frozen in place.

Waiting for a single terrible mistake in the potent spell being cast that would unleash it. Open the connection between this world and the very Abyss itself.

Free the Seven Kings of Hell into this world.

"It's as I feared," the Earth Wizard finally said, "Connie, we have little time to act and even less chance of salvaging the situation. An age or two ruled by the Darkest One may be the least of our worries soon ..."

"There's always a worse enemy," said Connie, "Eventually."

The Earth Wizard sighed.

But her quote did have too much truth in it.

"Yes," he said, "But if our new enemies win, I fear our world won't be around for the next enemies to appear."

Only due to his magic was he able to detect her sudden slight intake of air.

"I see," she said. And tightened the grip on her saber.

But its ability to cut through anything wasn't enough against the creatures she might soon face.

And again he hesitated to step inside. Her death if he died here was near certain. Although as a Paladin she vowed to fight to the death for him, she had lived a little more than two decades. Compared to his many millennia.

Using some power to drastically improve her chances of survival right now would reduce his drastically.

Yet his heart was too heavy, his conscious too leaden, to ever bring her into such mortal danger without some proper protection.

So he turned around.

Connie stiffened. Then began to turn –

"Wait," he said, "Hold your saber out to me."

She did. Careful not to point the tip at him. And twisted it so the flat faced him. The sharp cutting edges as far from him as possible.

He poked it with his finger. Muttered the ancient spells of light. Blessing the weapon against the darkest of darkness.

And it lit up with a mild warm glow now.

Connie gasped.

But this spell did the same as the three of the five glowing gemstones he had slipped into her pocket before they left. Even though the gemstones were currently shielded as best he could from any probes, physical or magical – but the moment Ash opened the letter, the shield would shatter, and the gems would reveal themselves to her –

When a big oily hand of cold seized him from behind.

Crushed down on him.

His blast of magic shoved Connie away.

Her gasped scream.

The crack of her boots landing several feet away.

"Go!" shouted the Earth Wizard, "I shall deal with –"

It yanked him inside.

The door slamming away any hint of light.

Into a broiling dark sea battering with oily ancient hatreds.

SIXTEEN

FELIX GOES WAR GOD

The shutters before Felix's gaze razored his sight. In the warm darkness he crouched. Ready to spring out of the cramped stone room three floors above the narrow cobble streets. The smell of brandy, cookies, and fear so thick he tasted it.

Let it fire up his blood.

The shrieks and snarls from the beasts below overwhelm the screams of the tormented dying. The clanks of solid black armor on those huge ratlings towering as high as the tall lampposts, if not several feet higher, were loud enough to crack the walls. Their huge swords and axes as big as an ordinary man. Carved wicked to bleed fear into their prey before bleeding life out of them.

With the full moon beaming, plenty of spidora bugs chattered on the rooftops, lycan swarming among their giant ratling brethren – the stink of rat, beast, and bug rise together in a gut-wrenching stench.

Yet it didn't disturb the lingering joy of the chicken broth and chopped noodles Grunts had served Felix.

None of those monsters deterred the Champion from the obvious route to attract the very vandread he now hunted. The two of the largest rats – each nearly a full nine feet high. Their black armor the thickest, spikiest, and with the largest axes each with twisted skulls for their double blades.

Yet none had bothered to raid the many buildings crowding the darklings together. Despite the streets barely fit the whole horde. As if the whole lot hadn't noticed the buildings. That plenty of humans hid quietly inside them. Praying silently that someone, anyone would save them from inevitable horrible death at the hands of these beasts.

All except this building.

Where only Felix stood on the third floor. Crouched.

Waiting for the right moment to strike.

His blade sheathed.

At the moment.

The two largest ratlings, shouting loudest in a harsh gibberish tongue. Clearly giving orders to the rest. Each with five hulking wolf lycan to guard them Plus, three giant ratling guards to each of the two largest ratlings – clearly two generals. Each ratling guard a foot shorter than the generals. Each armed with a matching broadsword or double axe.

When two of the ratlings guards positioned themselves right below Felix. Broadswords out and ready.

Felix flicked the shutters' lock open.

Hand flexed.

Breath quietly inhaled.

The two giant ratling general screamed their orders louder. Shook their massive fists high the air.

Then both turned away. Toward the darkling hordes if lycan, spidora, and ratlings roaring in the streets.

And Felix leapt out of the window.

Boots landing full force on the guards' heads. Down onto the armor.

Crushing them to the ground.

Killing them before they could scream.

Only letting his knees bend enough to ease his fall.

Grab their flying broadswords.

The wolf guards all turned. Howled. Charged.

And died.

Broadswords slicing them apart.

But another pair of the ratling guards leapt in front of their generals. Even if the rest of the darkling horde had frozen. Silent. Shocked at the mere human who dared strike at the very heart of their invasion.

An invasion that finally was cramped inside these narrow stone walls.

Where their numbers meant less.

Felix lunged at the ratling guards. The rats snarling. But their beady eyes wary of a human that could wield their huge weapons against them. The small distant in these streets an obvious disadvantage to them now.

Yet they raising their own axes. Ready to crush him. Their strength would certainly overwhelm him.

Or they definitely thought so.

But midway, Felix flung the broadswords right at them.

Both spun then smashed into their chests. Denting, then cutting into their armor. Knocking the two down, dead.

The two nine-foot generals charged at Felix. Axes raised high and fierce.

For no ratling worth more than a pack of bandits could take such a challenge to their authority without facing it down themselves.

Together the ratling general attacked like a whirlwind of black blades. Their axes hacking and slicing. The clanks of their boots against the cobble as sharp as their blades. No other darkling dare interfere. Dare try to show up their own generals.

The taste of blood and gore thick in the air.

Yet Felix merely dodged.

Not drawing his saber.

Not yet.

When the last two ratling guards struck from behind Felix. Their duty demanding it.

But their ratty stink, the screech of their armor, the whirl of their axes – it all gave them away.

And Felix drew his saber.

Ducked under the general's swings. Axes swooshing.

He slashed through their armor.

Through their chests.

Then their legs.

Their axes breezing past.

Till he slammed those blades with his free hand. Smashing them the heads of the ratling guards.

The ratling generals and their guards soon all crumbled dead. The silence as heavy as the black armor of every ratling here. The darkling horde stinking of the bitter fear they intended to raise out of their prey.

But Felix snatched one of the general's axes.

Flung it full force through the air above.

Slicing through several spidora leaping toward him. Cutting down the darklings who tried to ambush him from above.

Their vile purple blood spilling everywhere. Stinking up the air enough to sting Felix's eyes and nose.

Yet Felix merely turned toward the darklings hordes. Pointed his saber at them.

And said, "Who's next?"

They all howled.

Then all lunged to end him.

But Felix Stormbringer wouldn't fall here.

Because darkling blood would soon wash away all the human blood in Cheramin.

CHAPTER

SEVENTEEN

ASH, THE ANGUISHED DRUNK, PART II

Ash tasted his sweet Amber's cherry lips forever. Smooching their warm moisture. Moaning gently with her. Letting her savor his yearning for her every second since all those years ago.

Savor her yearning for him just as long ago.

Mouth to mouth.

The warm night as sensual and warm as the blood pounding through his veins. Heated by the buttery light of the lampposts. Giving everything, including her skin, a healthy extra gleam Amber usually needed a lotion to obtain.

With a milky tint added by that romantic moon. Perfect for any such climatic scene.

Even with the sounds of battle gone.

Replaced by moans.

And a couple gasps in a distance. Wet rips.

Without even a slight echo of our moans.

But bathing in her cherry and vanilla presence. A fragrance fit for a king. Or a wizard.

When a crack rang out. From the wine bottle he threw in the air. Smashing against the cobble.

Only then did he notice the touch of her fingers holding his jaw. And they were as warm as his cheeks.

Hot compared to the night.

He basked in her scent. That cherry vanilla as rich as her lips. Her breath carried it as much as her skin.

Yet he still held her left boob in his left hand. Squeezing that plump yet silky bulge of pleasure. The nipple poking his palm. His forearm pressed against the other divine, no, hellishly endowed bulge. Nipple covered and poking gentle through his coat too.

Till his Paladin training forced its way up. Well, enough to make him aware enough again to listen to his surroundings. The quiet growl of the lycan girls now a few feet behind him.

And still nothing else.

Besides his heart pounding hot chocolate through his veins. The fresh hot sweet chocolate only the best cafes could manage to stock.

It also demanded he stop groping his beloved babe of his dreams. Her inevitable slap would crack and echo across the entire zigzag of cramped streets. Warning every and any girl that Ash La Pushka was the biggest pervert of them all.

Yet every bit of him enjoy every perverted second of it.

At some point some well-meaning idiot would stumble up the empty street and get the very wrong idea. Gawk and scream. Try to pry them apart. Maybe notice her snake bone wings coming out of her back at some point too.

Maybe end up killed by Mandy or Snow. Ruining their bizarre drinking contest.

Because besting a vandread by drink – no way Mandy could top that.

And no way Amber, her playful mischievous self, wouldn't pass that chance up. At least for a good joke.

But this boob groping was part of her weakness as a vandread. Cutting the right strap, the right way too, probably. Certainly.

But the kiss?

His heart pounded even the hottest chocolate through my veins. Praying to any god anywhere, in Chemarin or not, would listen and this kiss would save them both.

Because the additional part of a vandread's weakness that switched her master was her ultimate secret. Any vandread's ultimate secret. Chosen exclusively by the vandread based on their weakness.

Something the magic of her existence prevented even her original master from knowing or acting on – which ended up doing the same protective act with the master who created her. Even if deep down she wanted to tell him, the magic compelled her to keep that part of her weakness utterly secret. Not even a subconscious hint. No matter how much she wanted to.

So if this kiss didn't do it, then ... well.

It's a been a nice fun life.

Ash broke off the kiss gently. Looked into her sad blue eye.

The lock of blonde hair curved over her left face still giving those juicy red lips and rosy cheeks a lovely haughty look of a young goddess about to meet her untimely end with devote grace and epic courage.

His heart raced quicker than a terrified rabbit dashing for its hole.

The words he had to ask, needed to ask, dangled on his tongue. Stubbornly clinging to it.

So, like usual, she spoke first.

"As romantic as getting my bare boobs groped suddenly is," she said, voice gentle and kind. Exactly *way* too gentle and kind for the content of her words.

Like talons snatching his heart.

Making him interrupt her before he could stop his blabbering mouth.

"But definitely the kinkiest, craziest weakness a vandread ever choose," he said, "That's what I love about you Amber. That and your drop dead gor–"

Amber shoved her forefinger across his lips.

Her silly grimace failed to lighten the stark silence of that moment.

Until a horrid inhuman screech blasted out from above.

A SCREAM LIKE a thousand nails against stone. Add a few hundred fish scrapped against rocks for good measure too. The cramped cobble echoing it against the cramped stone buildings. Making it even louder. Scratching every one of his bones raw.

Ash's instinct screamed to look up. Up at the sky. To scan for blocked stars.

Find the terrible source.

Right now.

His heart screamed to not look away from Amber. Her chest fruit still warmed his hand and arm. That cherries and vanilla presence too sweet to break from.

Especially when that silly grimace became a devious smirk.

"Yes, Master," Amber said. As mockingly and belittling to Ash as possible. That chin up and using her left lock of blonde hair to full haughty effect.

His heart ceased.

Or must of.

The world froze. His body ice. Pricks jabbing every inch of him.

Her master ... arrived?

A vandread like Amber was only mortal, fully helpless and vulnerable to fatal wounds, only while her weakness was exploited.

Meaning the moment he removed his hands from her boobs, she could, no, would slaughter him. A vandread by nature still needed to obey her orders. Staying alive to carry them out tended to involve destroying any idiot who discovered the weakness but failed to exploit it fully.

That's why his cowardly body suddenly demanded he slay

her. His Paladin instincts, those years of rough training, told him instantly the right move.

A good thrust in any vital would do it quickly.

Yet his heart screamed to let her go.

And his mind so horrified at his body's cold calculation that it kept him paralyzed for another vital moment.

When her sultry straps of doom swung up and behind her. Strung bloody through and around each lycan. Snow with it through her shoulders, stomach. Around her limbs.

And through her chest.

Blooding dripping out of her mouth. Eyes partly shut.

Across from her Mandy was the same – just the chest wound was below her boobs.

"Amber ..." he barely managed to stutter out.

"You smashed your chance, Ashtray, to little itty bits," said Amber, "First thing out of your mouth should of been an order to acknowledge you as my master. Then you should of given me my prime directive. But my original master got to me first so ... sorry, but the closing act's come and there's no delaying it much longer."

All he could do was gulp. His throat more bitter and sour than precious aged wine gone to vinegar – with rancid oil added for good measure.

Even if he still clung to Amber's chest fruit.

The night air seemed to grow horribly cold.

"Nooooo!" exclaimed a squeaky guy's voice. Coming quick from above. Behind Amber.

Suddenly a tabby kitten with bat wings zoomed at Snow.

Its tail ... an orange scorpion, including a barb that was probably poisonous.

It flew from some roof behind her. Darted around her moaning, bleeding body.

Like some horrified bizarre pet of the finest of nobles finally given an adorable voice.

"No, no, no," said the little bat-kitty, "I've worked so, so hard. You can't die now! It's not time –"

One of Amber's snake-bone wings flipped up. Looped around and plucked the bat-kitty from the air.

Then swung the gawking little critter where they both could see it clearly.

A bit scrawny. Fur a bit ragged. Smelling of little kitten too.

Especially with very wide, very sweet green grape eyes.

The kind of pathetic desperate grapes offered to a noble whenever a fool realized his horribly dire mistake, and adding the most heart-wrenching and sincerest of apologies with it.

Often losing their head afterwards, minus the torture beforehand.

Sometimes.

If they were lucky.

"Mercy! Mercy!" said the bat-kitty, "I'm just a harmless little manticore. Nothing to see here. I –"

That only made Amber raised her eyebrow.

"Since when did lycan keep pets?" asked Amber, "Or are you her mentor?"

"Pet?!" cried the bat-kitty, "I'm the great Leo – the little, unknown manticore named Leo. Just tagging along. Yeah, tagging along for –"

The snake-vertebrate bones tightened a bit.

And the bat-kitty squealed.

"Ack!" cried Leo, "I don't know anything! I didn't teach her any magic! I swear! I don't even know her! I mean, I only just met her ... recently. Let me explain."

Normally, at this moment, any sensible lightling or darkling would of started pointing out how horribly unbelievable and suspicious this squeaky bat-kitty sounded. Threatened some abuse in order to get it talking the truth.

But not Amber, or Ash.

Amber merely grimaced.

Ash's own lightly skeptical expression merely complimenting hers.

"Go on," she said.

Because acting this bad had its own charm.

"Well, where do I begin?" asked Leo.

"The beginning," said Amber, "Or course."

"Ah, yes, the beginning, of course," said Leo, "I was born the last of a lowly litter of manticores. Our nest was a squalid cave tattered with muddy dirt, broken stones, and chilly streams. Where my siblings beat me day and night. Me being the runt, of course."

"Of course," said Amber and me.

Because waiting for the right moment was key here. Even with the scent of blood growing so strong it started countering Amber's sweet cherry and vanilla scent.

Enough to chill any sensible fool's spine even more.

"The few mice and bunnies my poor, poor mom, thin and bony from hunger, managed to bring to us, oh how she struggled, she had to catch from long abandoned homes," said Leo, "And my dear siblings munched them all down. Every single one of them. Leaving none for me. You see, Bobby was a big manticore and needed to grow bigger. So did Bubba and Becky. But me? No. Not even a tail for me. Or a tiny bitty bone to gnaw. Or even a drop of blood to lap up. A runt stayed a runt. Their beatings bruising and bleeding me until I could take it no more! And I ran away. Across murky forests, smelly swamps, bone-dry deserts that nearly killed me. Until dying of exhaustion, my dear young Snow found me. Two little kids beat and shunned by everyone else. Her tale of woe even worse than mine!"

Now it was pretty hard for Ash to hide his shock. To the point his face ached from it. Because, while you hear of horrible liars all the time ...

But this horrible?

"Since you were little kids," said Amber, "Who met recently and shared heart-shredding tales of woe, and then gained unbreakable bounds of friendship. So I might as well shred both your hearts for real and end your mutual misery."

"Ack!" screamed Leo.

Then he screamed at Ash, "Go kiss her again! Order her to obey me! You! I mean –"

Amber blinked at the bat-kitty. Her juicy lips parted a bit. Skin paling a touch too.

Her body tensing. Even her boobs.

When I dove in and smooched her on the lips.

My mouth tasting her sweet, moist, warm cherry taste.

For only a moment.

Then Ash broke off and said, "Amber, I order you to –"

"Obey your original maker and –" interrupted Leo.

"But serve however you wish –" said Ash.

"But spare your original maker too –" broke in Leo.

"And follow your own heart," added Ash.

"As long as it doesn't involve killing me, the great Leonard," said the bat-kitty.

"Or –" Ash began.

But Amber shoved her palm over Ash's mouth.

Squeezed the bat-kitty so tight its bones should of cracked, even if there weren't any pop sounds. His squeal was only half its high-pitched intensity. Plus, very airy.

"You almost had me," said Amber, "A *second* time. Boys, this is getting ridiculous. Even for me. And that's saying *a lot*. It's been fun. And I do have one last question, Leo. If Gordack didn't make me, then why's he my master?"

Ash's own heart suddenly pounding hard at the news.

Gordack? The foremost Butcher Brother? Of the three toughest, cruelest ratlings for generations?

And a brilliant commander general supposedly too.

Even Felix wouldn't challenge them carelessly. Only an ambush, hidden by magical, could pull it off.

Except the eldest brother, rumor had it, had powerful magics at his command. Magics only the Earth Wizard could counter now, in person, according to the wizard's own random comments.

Now the stink of blood thick in the air made more sense.

The lamppost beginning to dim too. From so many late night, drunken experiences, these lights went out sometime between the next second and the next half hour or so.

Usually close, if not at, the worst possible moment.

Something Gordack must of planned for ahead of time.

And since Ash's memory after enough drinks wasn't all that reliable, it might be sooner.

Worse, everyone's fate was in the hands of a puny bat-kitty of legendary lying incompetence.

They were doomed.

"Well, you see," began Leo, "It's a long story. About a poor foolish wiz – boy – young man. Desperate for –"

Another squeeze and squeal shut the bat kitty up again.

"One last chance," said Amber, "Or I shred you *real* slowly."

Her wicked pearly white grin made Ash's hands *and* arms clammy. Despite her chest fruit warming them.

"Eeep!" said Leo, "Gordack –"

A preemptive squeeze and squeal cut him off. Sending his kitty head bobbling high up.

"The *truth*," said Amber.

"Yes, yes!" cried Leo, "Gordack wanted a vandread. Soul Magus too. He's quite a needy guy. And seeing how I specialize in undead, among other things, very expensive – ACK – okay. okay! I made lots of stuff during my illustrious career. But those two both refused to take the usual risks with vandread so he convinced me to try something interesting. Something that hasn't been done before. And I, the wonderful great prodigy Leonard, was up to the challenge. Because never-been-done-befores start getting rare after a while. Once you've lived long enough and so on. And an upset Gordack was the type to make sure I wouldn't live very comfortably for a very long. Not like the short stupid life of that poor brutish tig– I mean, spare dark ... lings, we memory hexed to –"

"Amber!" shouted Mandy, rasping loud, "I order you to spare our lives, hold that cat idiot tight, and find a safe way to heal me and Snow."

Amber gasped.

Blue eyes wide like struck by a blue bolt.

And said, "Yes, master."

Yet the tension in her body eased up a touch.

Her peachy complexion returned a bit.

Until her snake bone wings and sultry straps all suddenly shattered into nothingness.

THE CRACKLE of bone and strap shattering at once echoed too loud through the narrow streets. Freezing everyone. Only the dimming lights hiding the full extent of her wardrobe disaster. The two lycan trembling. Falling to the bloody cobble below them.

Landing each with a thump.

A wet gasp.

The clothing burst even hit Ash with a breeze of extra sweet cherry. Making the street a while seem even narrower.

The coppery blood made everything stink worse.

If people weren't staring through the dark, shuttered

windows on every floor, they definitely were now. Staying utterly silent too. With no lights to give them away.

No sane people here would draw attention to themselves during a darkling invasion.

When Leo squawked. Slipped free.

Wings flapping.

Until Amber grabbed him.

Smash his back against her stomach. Her left arm pinning the little kitten against her. Its head pillowed between her boobs.

And Leo now smiling perverted. Like a drunk groping his dream wench, a wench who willing playing along too.

"Didn't know you liked me this much," said Leo softly.

Too softly.

But Amber focused on Mandy. The orange tigress struggled to her feet. All her limbs wobbling. Bloody.

While Snow could barely get to her knees. The blood flowing freely.

Even from her mouth.

Enough to wrench Ash's gut. Technically, he shouldn't give a damn. His mouth shouldn't taste as sour as a lemon added to wine. No, he should cheer. Not only did Mandy just save his life. She would soon be dead. Her fox purren too. Then Amber and Ash would be free to abscond to a new life of playwrighting devilry.

Yay.

Ignore Mandy and Snow had fought beside him against Amber. Saved his pathetic life from an inevitable gruesome death.

"I know I place that might help," said Amber, "It's the only place we have a chance with too. A secret place. So you lycan better swear –"

"Take us," said Mandy, her three-inch claws coming out, "I order you to."

Amber clicked her teeth shut. Not quite bared them.

Though the twisting of her mouth suggested she really wanted to.

The silence surrounding everyone now thick enough that a bottle couldn't smash it.

"Fine," said Amber, "As you command, *master*. Just try to keep up. And not give us all away with trails of blood."

The catgirl's bloody grin sent several chills down Ash's spine.

Especially when her gaze landed on him.

"Two wins are mine," she said, "One more and you are mine as well."

Ash could only gulp at that.

Yet relieved that, as a man proud of his drinking process, demented him didn't just win by default.

EIGHTEEN

GORDACK HUNTING
DISASTER, AND DINNER

Gordack sniffed the hot night air. Heated with blood and death. The sweat of human fear and sweet flesh better than any pork. The stink of lycan fur and nipping bestial rage.

And the powerful biting aroma of rats.

The kind that made your eyes sting with tears of pride.

But the canyons these humans called roads in Chemarin were too scrawny for a ratling's body. The tiny stone buildings cramped too close together. The alleyways wouldn't even fit a full grown lycan. Maybe a tigress cub.

Maybe.

But those darklings spoiled their young too much to use them properly for war. Not much better than the humans who avoided using their young entirely for it.

His nine-foot frame packed with solid muscle and shielded by even more solid black armor took up too much space on these cobble roads. He even chose sword and axe so ridiculously short they hung off his waist.

But countering the lack of space here was critical enough to warrant it.

Despite how the cramped walls and the stone everywhere made his boots clank so loud any prey with functional ears could hear him coming miles away.

Well, if the Soul Magus hadn't cut off the natural echoing of the stone. The hex spell consumed the life of sound.

Preventing it from traveling too far. Making the city eerily silent, even here, despite his clanking boots, despite his horde preparing the next stage of the attack.

That cowardly wizard refused to show himself after all. Let his own city get razed to the ground rather than face defeat.

Gordack snickered.

Such behavior fit his own four-legged kindred.

The Soul Magus would soon have more than enough fresh corpses, lightling and darkling, to build the undead platoons needed for the next conquest.

And Gordack's own experiment, successfully planted, successfully kept secret, now reserved as backup for later, for when the Dreaded Ones inevitable began to turn on each other.

But first, for complete victory, two vital targets must be eliminated. The wizard and his boy. Unfortunately, the boy might be needed as a hostage first to draw out the Earth Wizard so with the Soul Magus' help, a trap had to be set. Several traps because prey rarely fell to lazy hunters.

His two wolf guards, listening to their rhythmic predictable step a few feet behind him to his sides, clearly only understand the hunter's perspective. Prey knew it needed to be unpredictable. Same for the orange tigress guard marching in a half-ready crouch, claws out and ready for battle, yet keeping the same few feet in front of him to his right.

Her eyes and head movement the same pattern.

Any ratling with a dozen years on his shoulder could slaughter this bunch of arrogant beasts.

When the tigress snapped her head up, Gordack watched her carefully. The smell of bitter fear coming off her confirmed his suspicion. The gasps of his wolf guards just proved they were as stupid as her.

Her death shriek cut off as she crumbled into ash.

The wolves growled. Claws definitely out. As if some enemy had attacked here.

Gordack chuckled.

The boy had taken the bait.

The tigress unaware of her bound to the vandread now died from losing it. Her soul torn from her, shredding her body to ash, and consumed by her lost slave. The other darklings as well. Punishment for their utter failure to eliminate the target in time.

The stupid cats thought the vandread belonged to Gordack. Due to a memory hex the Soul Magus implanted in their minds. Compelling them to give the vandread a standing order to obey and serve Gordack loyally as her master and perpetuate the apparent deception.

Then erased any memory of it from the cats' mind.

Serve the Ivy Reap right for her betrayal ... but her vixen purren ...her presence still considered him.

The vandread played along quite well. Her acting skills and flare for the dramatic ... horribly impractical for real combat yet amazing useful in the most unexpected ways. Her passion for it too. One of the few darklings who thought beyond bloodshed and death.

And one that had a real future.

Not to mention that strange sweet smell of hers. That clean lush appearance that made his mouth water for roasted human girl. Losing such a unique vandread and letting the enemy obtain her ...

No.

If sacrificing that darkling was the only reliable way to eliminate the boy and wizard, then the price was worth it. Nothing else would better guarantee a total victory than their deaths. A vandread couldn't be the prophesized darkling to transcend the darkness anyway.

Whatever transcending the darkness meant.

It was the boy that the doomseers claimed would one day pose the greatest threat.

Doomseers who had to watch their brethren die painfully before they spoke remotely clearly.

That seer in that human temple ... a prize definitely worthy claiming and protecting soon.

Maybe breeding with too.

And with enough coin, a few clear threats, and those so-called priestesses would sell the seer to him.

No need to waste time and soldiers crushing them.

This inter-shade trade, as the Duke BloodTalon called it, might have some benefits, after all.

But nothing the stupid lycan would understand. His stupid wolf guards kept sniffing the air. As if they didn't notice Gordack's own calm and collected scent. One decent sniff with their broken short too human noses would tell them her death was expected.

A good sign, in fact.

The dark-skinned human of decent fighting prowess should be close. One of the last defenders of the city. The man was definitely a Champion. Probably the only one who hadn't run up north to die by the hands of Gordack's mentor at Storm Killer.

And if left alive might delay the invasion too long for the Soul Magus' great hex over the city to activate properly.

Once Gordack dealt with the Champion, victory would soon be complete.

And the Champion's red-haired girl would serve as a great roasted feast to celebration the first and most critical victory of the War of Light.

Her and that yellow-skinned girl dressed like the Champion.

A tasty exotic reward for sending that other white fox lycan, one uncovered by careful questioning, after the yellow-skinned one ...

His chuckle was so intense that Gordack almost missed the dark-skinned Champion dash across the next intersection.

Only a few dozen feet away.

The soft echoes of the Champion's boot were already getting consumed by the Soul Magus' sound-killing hex. The puny stone buildings were barely able to echo a single sound anymore. The oil in the lampposts would die in another hour too. Leaving the city in the dim light of the full moon.

Putting the remaining humans at an even greater disadvantage.

Including the Champion.

But Gordack needed the Champion dead as soon as possible. With the grand hex the Soul Magus was finalizing, any delay could spell disaster for all life for miles around.

So Gordack sucked in a giant breath.

When his red-haired prey swaggering to the intersection moments afterwards. Then her awkward speed tripping her. The girl squeaking. Landing with an awkward thump.

Her sword flying a vertical arch toward Gordack.

Landing far closer to Gordack than the human girl.

The Darkest Gods were truly with him and his hordes tonight.

His shrill bellow caught the attention of the red headed prey. Her gasp and gawk paralyzing her as planned.

His sprint carrying him quick to seize his prize.

Quicker than his whimpering wolf guards could match.

The red headed girl gasped again as he closed in.

Jumped away.

Like a little helpless bunny jumped away the grizzly bear looming inches above it.

His claws seized her. Crushing her and her limbs tight enough to fracture. Her scream. The cracks.

Yet she snarled at him. The alcohol on her breath stung Gordack's eyes back enough to require a blink or two.

"Ash!" she hissed, "What did you do to Ash?!"

That perked his ears up as much as her tasty scent lifted his nose.

Prey that had valuable information *and* value as a hostage.

"Ash La Pushka ..." Gordack said. Letting the drooling from tasting her roasted body in the future drip out a bit. "Yes. That target ..."

And chuckled knowingly.

Her eyes bulged as if he had plucked out one of her teeth.

If only she could hear all the screams and cries of her kind dying too.

"He's not ... noooo!" the girl wailed.

Bait for another trap, no, a better double trap now unfolding right before his eyes.

And exactly what he had hoped for. More than he dared wish for.

The Darkest Gods truly were look down on him tonight.

NINETEEN

SNOW LOST BUT FOOLISHLY FOUND

The winding streets were as twisty and wrecked as the bleed gash through her chest. Her legs wobbled as flimsy as the plate of overcooked noodles the city designers used as a blueprint for these roads.

It didn't help that the tall buildings were so cramped together.

They might as well have been chunks of venison smothering in brightly covered spices only those who imagined themselves immensely rich bothered with. The kind of people who then paled at the price of an exotic fox lycan after Snow put on the usual show demanded by her human masters.

The rough uneven cobble jabbed the pads on her paw feet. Numbing despite the uneven slabs of cobble.

Yet oversensitive to the sharper stabs.

Funny how several open and bleeding gashes throughout

your body could make you both too numb to some stuff like the humid breeze, to every prick on your feet, but overly sensitive to every aching muscle and gash.

Her toe claws caught so often in some random unseen crack that Snow normally would of seen and avoided that she had no idea why they hadn't broken to crumbly bleeding pieces by now.

Well, except maybe she didn't have the strength to break any of them.

Yet.

The dark plum pudding sky above didn't seem to hide any watchful eyes. No unexpected deviations on the roofs from slanted tiles and half-open piping to catch the rain. Nothing peeping out from the tiny alleyways. But those alleys were so narrow she couldn't squeeze her furry butt through them entirely even when she was in good health.

So the spidora hadn't caught up yet.

Why?

Their lycan blood trails were clear enough for anyone to follow, even anyone only slightly capable of sight or smell. The moon above was so fat and full it already gave everything a milky cast. Enough to see that their paths circled and interweaved.

Because her sense of smell easily work out which blood trail in the gory streets was their own fresh trail.

Plenty of bodies sprawled here and there, mostly human and young, to hide anything that passed much beyond a few minutes ago.

The dimming lampposts would only help her darkling brethren finish their dirty job they started tonight.

Her spell hiding the humans from her brethren would soon fade. Her strength no longer enough to maintain it.

That she lingered far in back of this odd group didn't help her case either. The nutcase duplicate Amber led right ahead of Mandy. How neither Ash or Mandy noticed that that nutcase was a duplicate, a fake … but Snow didn't have the strength to groan.

Instead, her treacherous stomach fluttered. As if the maggots that would soon feed on her flesh had preemptively hatched into butterflies and clustered themselves cozy all there.

Her gaze lingered too often on Ash, not on the arrogant tigress stumbled alongside him. Bleeding everywhere like her poor foolish vixen purren. Huddled over as little as possible, to prove to the corpses that tigress … well …

Snow sighed. Too much blood loss.

Her own movements were too jerky. Poorly hiding her injuries. Mandy wasn't doing much better. She only tried to act that way.

If Mandy died, that nutty vandread – who knew what would happen? Yet as long as Mandy lived, Snow had to serve as her purren.

While Ash kept just in arms' reach of Mandy and Amber...

Barely.

But the fact the spidora hadn't caught up by now meant they planned something far more horrible than merely running everyone down, wrapping them in webbing, then implanting eggs inside that would hatch and eat each of them alive – eventually taking over their bodies and minds and transforming everyone into new spidery monstrosities.

Yet no one but Snow seemed to remember her healing magic. Mandy must really underestimate Snow's healing talents. That walking all this way let her recover enough strength to attempt heal to herself properly.

It didn't vanquish the wounds right away.

Gashes shrank to cuts. Then down to slits. Then healed. Like an invisible forced pushed them together,

Fusing them back to normal.

Holes closed over. Insides repaired. Knitting together. Growing as itchy, no, more itchy, than when Snow had to wear human clothing over her fur.

A few moments later the aches and pain vanished too. Then the itching.

Leo, in fact, did teach her some useful magic. Helped her sorry butt escape from the pelt farms. His terms would come later. A few missions, a bit unpleasant in some ways, he claimed, probably somewhat honestly too.

Not that she would use another of her magical tricks, a slow swipe of her hand and it would vaporize the blood and gore off her fur.

No, she pretended to limp. As if still wounded.

Since if Mandy discovered Snow's talents ...

Wait. If Mandy died, Ash would win by default. He, deep down, hated winning by default. Not the non-cheating, cheating sort of win.

And the vandread, a change of ownership shouldn't of caused any remarkable change in its form. That it's wings and straps shattered ... very unusual. According to what Leo taught her. If this vandread wasn't made like the usual ones, which according to Leo, it probably wasn't ...

Would this fake Amber die too? Ash definitely loved that dangerous blonde nutcase. It was too much like Snow herself before her purren hellmare. Lycan did *not* appreciate play-wrighting, plays, or actresses the way humans did. Causing whole human slave rebellion thing ... Snow was lucky she wasn't killed. Leo created a duplicate body just in time for Black Fang to assassinate a sleeping fake.

Not that Snow could explain any of this to Ash. Amber a darkling spy? One of the very lycan that ravaged his home city?

Better that he embraced that fake than discover the truth.

So timing here was everything.

The moment Mandy passed out; Snow had to rush to heal her just enough to keep her alive. Without waking her.

Because if Mandy passed out, it clearly was Ash's victory. Drinking contests typically got won that way.

Then Snow could bargain with him. Use Felix's passphrase and gain her freedom.

Leave out her past as Amber.

Maybe he'd even let her join their Paladin group. Grow to trust her. Even uncover the truth when he was ready for it, ready to forgive what her darklings masters insisted she do. Mandy would need help adjusting to human society. A fellow lycan that understood both reasonably well ... one that was genuinely willing to help her ...

So Snow scanned the nearest buildings one more time.

Then back at Ash.

Who stood facing her. Amber and Mandy to his right.

And fox lycan to his left. Fur coat colored and as beautiful as Snow's. Holding a pale blue saber arched back casually, its blade carefully pressed against the right side of his throat.

While Ash's saber remained sheathed. His hands stiff and far from it.

The fox lycan smirked wicked at Snow.

"Obey me or he dies," she said. Her voice as soothing warm and slick as an oiled needle through her skull. "Then the rest of you will die even slower, my dear little cubling."

Snow gasped.

Insides wrenching.

Then nodded.

"Clean yourself off," the new fox lycan said.

A simple swipe of Snow's hand magicked the blood and gore away. Made it blow off and crumble like paper burning away till none remained.

Mandy's scowl burned as much as stepping on a bit of fiery coal.

"Now come over here," the new fox lycan said.

And Snow obeyed.

Walking till she stood a few feet from the newcomer. Where she could smell her scent. A gentle yet mild foxy scent that reminded her a bit of her dear sister Scarlet so long ago.

Yet her very presence seemed to weigh Snow down harder than any steel cage made of the heaviest metals.

That evil grin ... that presence ... both grew the moment a terrible thought crossed her mind.

Confirming the horrible truth.

"Azura Snow," she said, "I'm so disappointed in you."

She was the Darkest Fourth.

"And you should never disappoint your mother."

CHAPTER

TWENTY

GORDACK, CLUTCHING
VICTORY BY THE THROAT

If the Darkest Gods bothered to peer into the narrow canyons these lightlings called streets, inhaled the aromas of fresh blood and gore congealing on the cobble, and drooled over the numerous corpses soon to be brought back to life –

Gordack chuckled.

How many more dead bloodied in the insides of the shuttered buildings. Too cramped together to provide necessary escape routes. No. They simply barred them inside. Penned them.

Whole families for slaughter.

Their crude pine furniture wasn't even worth chopping into firewood. Their ragged fabrics, the curtains and covering, so poor quality they weren't even worth gathering as loot. Forget the rotten fruit and vegetables they saved to throw in with barely edible meats long since spoiled.

The iron lampposts were now dark enough. No ordinary lightling could see their enemies coming for their lives. The dim and fading lights only help the few true lightling warriors.

Warriors that his darkling soldiers had long since massacred.

Except for the dark-skinned Champion still running through the streets. Hopefully hacking away at forces that would eventually overwhelm him. The endless maze of winding roads only served to aid ratlings corner and trap the few foolish lightlings left as they lost themselves in the darkness.

The full moon above sweetening the entire scene with its dim milky light.

Yet only his two remaining wolf lycan bodyguards here to celebrate the victory. Both too stupid to realize the war had been practically won tonight. They still crouched and sniffed the humid bloody air. Their wolf stink spiced with the raw fear from the unexpected sudden death of their tigress companion.

But Gordack would soon send those worthless mutts to their deaths.

A proper death due to their utter failure to protect him against Black Fang's obvious assassination attempt so long ago.

Gordack wouldn't dull his axe and sword with such worthless prey either.

Not even the current ridiculously short set hanging off his waist.

The redheaded girl moaned in his massive hand. As if her cries would stop him from crushing her slender frame. That he would stop before her struggle was barely felt from his furred pads.

His thick black armor already helped hide his giant nine feet of brawn and claws. His glare from powerful red eyes. Trim yellowed fangs grinning at her in inevitable victory. The thought of roasting her in blood gravy spiced with lead already making his mouth water.

Plus the golden ear rings in his knotted ears ...

The little glint from the moonlight should give the lightling girl just enough hints to direct the fear that drenched her sweet stink bittersweet.

Yet she directed her gaze at his broad chest plate.

If he didn't know better, she was staring at the black maroon rune shaped like a fat backwards S and painted as a serpentine rat. A special crest endowed with magics best not spoken of for risk of enemies figuring out its true powers.

To risk even thinking of.

The huffy pout on her lips. Bulging those cheeks.

It made his tail arc higher.

Almost trigger the poisoned barb on his tail's steel claw.

"Who drew that atrocity?" she asked, "It looks familiar. The style. Had to be the same lousy artist bastard."

His grin twisted into a growl.

"The best," Gordack hissed. Then squeezing the human girl harder. "Any insult to it is an insult to the Soul Magus' judgment. For he called its creator among the greatest of his kind."

"More like greatest manure pile of his kind," she said, "But

I'm sure where there's a will, there's delusion. Just ask Ash – ack!"

Gordack crush the girl in his massive hand. His claws ached to drive themselves deep into her unprotected flesh. Her flimsy cotton shirt and trousers worthless against any of his fangs or claws. Worthless against any of her own kind's dull weapons.

That cherry stink of hers finally grew a proper bitter tone of fear.

Her whimpers dying off. Roasting her unconscious would not be as satisfying.

His own magics could waken her and keep her awake when the time was right to punish her for her foolish words.

"Chop the oink-oink," said the redheaded girl's voice.

But from slightly over a dozen feet ahead of him.

Not from the girl in his hand.

"And listen to my firing ram!" shouted the distant girl.

Gordack looked up.

Just in time to see a navy-blue sole smash his nose.

And its neon blue leather boot twin slam its heel into the side of his snout.

Before stars and pain engulfed his world in bloody copper red.

His world clear only a slow painful moment later.

But not until that howls of his lycan bodyguard warned

Gordack of another enemy. The crack of stone, the lycan's dying screams from – both came from the wall of a nearby building. His nose too clogged with fresh blood to let him sniff out the danger.

But Gordack bared his fangs and sucked in the humid hot air. The fruity stink of the redheaded girl even stronger now. Well over the rich smells of gory conquest.

As if she was the one who kicked him.

But how?

The girl within his massive hand still resisted the clenching of his fingers. Her soft flesh and fragile bones bending and creaking.

Even as he regained his footing, Gordack blinked away the starry shock that blinded him for a moment.

But not before the girl in his hand suddenly vanished. As if she turned into thin air.

Then the crack of boots hitting cobble signaling the bitch was running away.

Enough to make Gordack roar.

Leap, turning to pursue.

But someone yanked his tail back.

Cutting Gordack's giant leap into a mere step.

When his vision fully cleared.

The redheaded girl ran quicker than any ordinary human. Far enough away that a pursuit would be worthless now. Dressed in what could only be called neon blue underwear with a skirt so short it could only be called unfinished – it revealed her figure was now even more slender and curvy than before.

That peachy unmarred skin ... his tongue drooled over its crisp roasted taste sweetened properly by lead and a few drops of cyanide.

But meaty hands clamped down on his tail midsection.

Gordack swirled around.

Roaring.

Snatch his sword.

Swinging it at the enemy at the enemy who dared challenge him.

While triggering the poison dart on the tip of his tail. Then letting it hang loose.

The target – a huge human man. A small wall of dark brawn. Dressed in the outfit of a Paladin.

The Paladin champion.

His savory smell – of healthy muscle and skin at peak condition.

The sneer on his square face would soon grow dull from death.

Yet the Paladin crouched. Planting his boots more firmly on the cobble.

Whipped out a puny thin saber at Gordack's thick short sword.

A crack erupted.

Red sparks flying.

And Gordack's blade was stopped mere feet from the human's smirking head. Blocked by the flat of the Champion's blade. While the sharp tip pointed right at his heart.

And only a several feet away.

But rumor had it the blades of Paladins could pierce any

armor less thick than the blade itself. Observations of Champions' armor and weapons hacked through with a single slice, with strength unheard of, impossible for humans ...

So Gordack snatched his axe.

Swipe an upper cut from the side. At the man's vulnerable gut.

The human should of jumped back. Retreat a safe distance.

But no.

The champion lunged at Gordack. Blade scrapping against blade.

His saber thrusting right toward a fatal heart stab.

Until Gordack flicked his tail's barb straight into the champion's back. Plunging deep.

Through cloth, flesh, and bone.

Injecting the fatal poison.

Yet the Paladin continued to charge. Too close too quick. Gordack's weapons couldn't counter this close.

Those leather boots cracked against cobble like a miniature troll. Saber tip mere feet –

Then inches from Gordack's own chest.

The man's eyes as dark as the night around him.

As determined as a bolt shot fired straight into a lava beast.

And for once in his existence, the ratling's blood ran cold. Like a river of frozen acid. Certain his black armor wouldn't stop this blade from ending his career.

When the life suddenly vanished from the man's eyes.

And the Paladin collapsed dead.

Gordack didn't know how long his heart then pounded in his hearts.

Or how long he chortled at his incredible luck.

But he did know that this vile corpse would soon prove to become his greatest undead creation yet.

CHAPTER

TWENTY-ONE

ASH, DESPERATELY DOOMED

Ash don't know what twisted his gut more – the scent, the sight, the tickle of blood and gore covering Mandy and Snow, it all suddenly vanishing into thin air, or how milky the moonlight made Snow as she trembled at the sight of her very evil mother behind him.

The lampposts were dim enough that the details of the buildings were engulfed by darkness. The utter silence of everything – from down the maze of roads and alleyways, from the many shuttered windows, from even the far distance …

It sent so many chilly zips up his spine he almost shivered – except the sharp edge of the blade pointed pressed against him stopped the foolish movement dead cold.

Because he headed toward dead cold.

That the crackle of the blood and gore crumbling into nothingness was so low yet somehow so loud …

188

He nearly shuttered. Again.

The taste of alcohol burned the back of his throat ragged. No way anyone inside those buildings were watching without feeling the same creeping, slimy feeling inside their guts. Racking their bones with even more chills.

But then again, with all the blood, gore, and bodies sprawled on the streets on the way here, maybe no one else was left alive.

Every few feet, another victim or two. The bumpy cobble guttering the congealed blood as wretched as vomit from a drunk about to faint. Occasionally a broken blade tip some-where. More than rattling's pile of cracks plank wreckage from stands or wagons utterly destroyed by giant clubs or axes.

All enough to make Ash question his ridiculous drinking contest with Mandy.

Had he slit her throat when he had the chance ... would he of managed to kill a few more darklings in time to spare a few more lives? Given a few of the now dead victims a chance to escape to the sprawling forests of dense entangled cathedrals oaks and thorny mattresses of blueberry brush beyond the giant stone walls surrounding this city?

That Mandy and her wide poison ivy eyes gawked wide at the sight of Snow.

And Snow's bloodthirsty mother behind Ash.

Even Amber herself must of feared this bloodthirsty lycan. Her once sweet cherry scent was fouled by raw bitter fear.

The bat-kitty smushed against Amber's chest was barely able to let out a scared squeak.

So when Snow trudged up Ash. Gazed at her mom blue eyes sharp yet full of terror.

Ash decided the silence was too much.

"Um," He began to say.

"Shut up," said Snow's mom, "Or die sooner than planned."

He did.

Shut up, that was.

But a glance toward the new villainess revealed she was a fox lycan like her daughter. With a fur coat similar to Snow's. Her almond face and lovely figure far too similar to Snow for coincidence. Even her white hair and its blue highlights was uncanny in its resemblance.

Her scent suddenly hit his nostrils.

Underneath the blood and gore was a bit of rosy jasmine fragrance. Sending his heart racing for some reason.

Even his mouth rushed to obey too.

Ash couldn't open it even if he wanted to now.

"To reduce yourself to a mere purren," said Snow's mom, "Do you know the effort I went through to ensure the right raising ritual? Completing it properly would have granted you nearly as much strength and power as I have now. Even in its current state, it increased your strength and abilities greatly ..."

The silence pause sharpening the blade of the next obvious words.

"Yet you throw it all away to help some pathetic Champion and his little construct," said Snow's mom. The acid in her voice could melt through several feet of steel.

"Um, what?" asked Ash.

The blade nipped the right side of his throat.

Snow frowned. Her pose stiffer than a prisoner about to executed.

The scents of every else but Snow's mom fouled by even rawer fear.

"Last warning, boy," said Snow's mom, "Speak once more unbidden and you die."

Ash opened his mouth to concur.

Then shut it and gulped.

Not even daring to nod.

"Good," said Snow's mom.

"Mom," said Snow, "I –"

The newcomer huffed.

About as scornful as Connie during Ash's usual nonsensical drunk rants that he thankfully, rarely, remembered after the hangover the next day.

If only Connie forgot them as well.

And the exact kind of scorn nobles from his mother's rival families threw at each other all the time. At her too. For being the spawn of a rival family and having the blood of a common solider. As if the blood from theirs didn't count at all.

"Shut up," Snow's mom said, "Hiding so many humans from the darklings here – you truly thought no one would notice it. A spell here. A spell there. Then a massive link covering the whole city. Until the lightlings hidden in their homes gave off no scent or sound. As if darklings were *stupid* enough not to check them?"

That dropped Ash's jaw as much as it didn't Snow's.

Saving Felix?

Then saving plenty of civilians?

Suddenly, Snow was looking incredibly beautiful for a fox girl. Enough that he could enjoy her lady bits, the silky white fur over the, *and* the blue highlights emphasizing them.

Ash would win her freedom.

Somehow.

And even make him curious what her face looked like without the fur covering it. Her body too.

"So unbelievably foolish," said Snow's mom, "A few lessons from a bunch of backwater hedge mages ruling a backwater kingdom and you think you're ready for the grand stage. Even Scarlet soon realized her lessons from her wizardly guardian were sorely lacking."

As much as it twisted his gut, that backwater stuff made an odd sort of sense. The lessons from his own wizardly father were lacking too. That the Four Realms was a backwater place and its wizards weren't as amazing as they seemed ...

Ash wondered what kind of world existed beyond the Four Realms.

Whether the tall cramped buildings here, with their bright painted decorations, would seem as primitive as huts.

Whether the minced meat pies and fountains of alcohol were old-fashioned and crude.

What they would think of this crazy War of light and Darkness.

Especially how it supposedly happened every age or so. Regularly too from the sound of it. Just destroy enough history books over the years and no one would remember enough of the ancient past to connect the knots either.

"Scarlet?" said Snow. Her face beginning to light up. Fear and hope twisting it. "She –"

"She's alive," said the newcomer lycan, "Different name. Earned herself the right to spent a few years at Darkheart. A magical school where she will receive a *proper* magical education. Where I'm sending you, but with far less –"

"But –" began Snow.

"No butts except yours heading to Darkheart right now," said Snow's mom, "Right after I slice open the throat of this boy with the right ritual and take his talent for myself."

Dying here.

With the lamppost were so dim they were practically out. The silence so unnaturally complete it sent a few extra shivers up his spine.

Bad enough the bright milky moonlight from the giant full moon was the only reason Ash could still see at all.

See the shock on Snow's face. Those crisp blue eyes. As blue as the electric icy bolt she could create out of thin air. With friendly cheeks dimpled pleasantly, despite her shock and fear tensing froze in a half-gawk, jaw hanging expression.

If only he could see Amber's. Her electric blue eye might not be so haughty but ...

Electric blue eye ...

Snow's face ... those lips, turn them juicy cherry red, throw her long hair over the left side of her face, minus the fur and add a crisp peachy complexion ... and her body, those ratios Penny obsessed too much about, even the slight curl of her slim hands ...

So much like Amber ...

But he didn't dare look toward the vandread Amber to compare. Warn Snow's mom of Amber's value, or the connection he was wondering about, of Amber possibly being Snow's secret sister.

That mind-bending jasmine stink failed to hid Amber's sweet cherry aroma too.

As if some furball could out do Amber.

Other than Snow, of course.

Who already succeeded in reaching hero-status within a real-life play situation. Hopefully, this play has a happy ending.

But the tragic one seemed inevitable.

Yet his heart still pounded strong. Her dear Amber might still have a chance for a second life. A second chance to become the greatest playwright ever. Snow, as the look-alike daughter of this villainess and his beloved, would probably survive scolded but not out.

Down but not out.

Two opposite sides uniting –

A desperate scheme flushed his blood as hot and sweet as hot chocolate touched with vodka.

"I'll marry Snow," Ash said, "My latent talent, rare and powerful, combined with her, um, potential ... our children should prove –"

When agony slice down the right side of his throat and across his chest. Wetness pouring out of the crack of pain.

And Ash fell on his ass.

Then collapsed on his back.

Panting.

"A lesson for you, my dear Snow," said her mom. The curved blade bloody now.

And Ash's body too weak to stand back up.

Snow glanced terrified at him.

Her foxy ears clearly sinking at his inevitable death.

"Disappoint me at Darkheart ..." she continued.

"I'll do my best, mother," said Snow. Her hands huddling low below her waist.

"But if Ash truly has such rare and valuable potential," Snow said, "Then –"

But Snow's mother growled like a pitbull denied his long-awaited steak bone.

The silence of the city so heavy it echoed her menace perfectly.

"Any other witch so arrogant as you would suffer greatly at my hands," Snow's mother said, "Beg for death. Which I would only grant after I tire of punishing her. By ripping out their liver, lobe by lobe, and eating it raw. Letting her feel my fangs sink into her flesh and chew it apart. Spiced bittersweet by her fear and despair. Then followed by whichever organ I am in the mode for. Until I am full of my feast and I let her die.

And that, my dear daughter, is why you should keep your claws and fangs as sharp and trim as possible."

That made everyone else gasp. Then gulp out loud. Ash. Snow. Mandy. And Amber.

All at once.

The oppressive silence ... the quiet echoed even louder than the menacing growl before.

Especially when Snow's mom lunged at Snow.

Shoved the blade into her gut.

Ripping it up. The wet sound of flesh and bones sliced apart slowly.

The pain twisting Snow's face.

When Snow's mom yanked the blade out. Grabbed her daughter's shoulder.

Then flung her toward Ash. Beside him.

Snow's bloody gasp ending when she crashed down beside him. A whimpering moan escaping her lips as she turned her head at him.

"Sorry," she said, "If only ..."

That expression ... so much like Amber as she died so often in her favorite plays ...

But Ash rubbed her elbow. Enough strength remained for that.

Her fur was as soft and silky as it looked. Strange how much that comforted him.

"You tried," he said, "I'm sorry for –"

A weak ack rang out from Mandy.

Snow's mom had plunged her blade into the catgirl's gut. Ripping it up to her chest.

Then flung her down hard to the ground. Her body cracking against the cobble.

Landing beside Ash. His other side.

Coughing up bloody gasps.

Amber cried, "Master!"

Before Snow's mom grabbed her boob. Pressed her forearm against the other.

Then plunged the blade up diagonal through Amber's side. Till the tip broke through her opposite shoulder.

Her electric blue eyes foggy with fear.

Ash's throat too tight to speak.

"You're no longer needed," said Snow's mom, "Fade out now."

And her eyes turned empty.

Face lifeless.

"As you command," Amber said. No emotion in her dead voice.

Then Snow's mom ripped the blade out. Flung her body down beside gagging Mandy.

But after the thump, Amber didn't move at all.

Yet Ash could find the strength to stand back up. His legs too weak to listen. His arms barely able to rub Snow's elbow anymore.

When a familiar roar erupted what had to be a dozen feet behind Ash.

"What did you do to him, you bitch!" screamed Penny.

TWENTY-TWO

ASH, DRUNKEN FAILURE

At the screech of Penny's voice, Ash gasped. Heart leapt pumping cherry sweet.

Who else but that redheaded pigtailed nutcase of a beauty would save his stupid ass here? With streets full of corpses and blood. As full as blood as the back of his gurgling throat. The air so thick with the stink he could taste it too. Along with too much of his own blood. Lampposts so dim any monster could strut up to your face and eat you whole before you knew it.

Or a stone wall could mug you and get away with it, no witnesses either. The painted fruits and other doohickies weren't about to start talking. Not with them splattered with so much blood they couldn't see anything if they wanted to. The shuttered windows were still dark.

Anyone inside long since hidden.

Definitely praying they would survive, no darkling would

find them, sniff them out, wondering who this Snow lady was who somehow hid them, if she still hid them, what her connection to these invading darklings were.

Hoping she wasn't one of them, about to betray them or something.

But if they survived, Snow and everyone else somehow survived, would these civilians speak up for her once they discovered she was a domesticated lycan, an exotic vixen breed? Would they back her up her when the rest of the city's survivors demanded her death to pay for the deaths of their own kindred, their friends, their livelihoods?

Pay just like the few other surviving darklings would.

Ash, as the only son of the Earth Wizard, as an established Paladin even if his reputation was less than stellar, he could save Snow if he managed to survive. Convince the Earth Wizard to acknowledge her as a potential Paladin, let her go to the academy, with a good recommendation even ...

No doubt she'd face some skepticism.

Okay, more than skepticism. But the wizard's word backing up Ash's should stem the worst of it.

Give her a chance to prove herself.

Mandy ... maybe. If he was feeling particularly generous, and the catgirl was honestly willing, backed by oaths, and she promised to return the favor properly.

Better than that ridiculous purren nonsense.

Assuming Penny didn't just kill Mandy and Snow after saving him. Slit their throats or something.

Just to be on the safe side.

Had Ash dared to look Penny's way, he was sure properly.

she would be branding her blade. Making sure she appeared as menacing as a black thundercloud throwing its mightiest tornado at the most arrogant rover's ply wood tents in the middle of Tornado Plains during the Tornado Season.

Even if their thieving Rover God stood right in her way.

Well, until she said, "I'm the only one allowed to torture him! *Ever!*"

Ash could only grimace at Snow. Rub her elbows some more as she lay flat on her ruined stomach. Cringing in obvious agony. Blood pooling underneath her. Staining her pristine white fur and its lovely blue streaks.

She even smiled back.

One that reached those warm blue eyes. One so much like Amber's.

Her face ... minus the fur ...

Exactly like Amber's. Her voice ...

His clenched suddenly stammered.

"Snow ..." Ash whispered, "You're Amber ... aren't you?"

But her eyes turned empty.

His insides crashing landing, as if plunging deeper than the deepest chasms, through solid rock, ripping it apart.

All he could do was turn to Mandy. Hope he was so very, very wrong.

She squinted one poison ivy eye at him. Grimace.

Even if both were softened by a touch of sweet friendly grape.

Softened further by a weak smile.

"So you never knew ..." A purr weaker than her smile hummed form her.

His expression stabbed his own face.

"It was a good match," she said, "I would of won ... if the Darkest Fourth hadn't interfered. Dishonored our contest. So I admit my defeat. Sorry that I couldn't ..."

The life in her eyes suddenly gone too.

The horrible chuckle erupted out of Snow's mom. One that drew Ash's full attention.

The vicious lycan looming a couple feet before his boots. Her blade raised and ready for its next victim, a certain nearby redhead.

"Then you can join him," said Snow's mom.

"Why you!" exclaimed Penny.

The cracking stomp meant only one thing. Her boots pounding the cobble. Ready to charge an instant later. A charge this evil lycan would expect.

But not the zigzag Penny would toss in at the end. Ash hid his grim smile as a frown. Revenge wouldn't bring Snow, or Amber, or even Mandy back. Just bring closure.

A cold comfort, but better than nothing.

Until Penny screamed out wild in pain.

And a thump erupted a couple feet from his head. And a moan and whimper, one that Ash recognized as Penny's.

"Ash ..." Penny said, "I'm sorry. I thought ... that ratling ... was-"

And silence again.

Yet Ash's hands refused to even clench shut hard into fists. A failure to the end.

"Gordack," said Snow's mom, "What wonderful timing. You may enjoy these fresh corpses as you wish. The boy's too."

"Thank you, Darkest Fourth," said Gordack. The harsh voice coming from less than a dozen feet behind Ash. "I'll leave the last Champion to you, if you wish. They hid her well. Not even her Paladin companions knew of her rank. Dress like the boy, she's an exotic human girl with a flat face and yellow skin. A gift for your generosity."

The Darkest Fourth? The fourth strongest of the five Dark Ones? A being only a wizard could counter. Even the greatest of Champions needed the aid of a wizard against them.

Something even Felix reluctantly admitted during his drunkest moments.

Yet the vicious fox lycan merely turned away. Began strolling down the gore-ridden street as if it were a beautiful garden.

Her bloody blade an umbrella over her shoulder. Ready to spike any enemy to fall upon her.

Yet nothing Ash could do but bare his teeth at her. His body already growing numb. Too weak to even rub Snow's corpse anymore.

He couldn't even feel the jagged cobble underneath his back.

What did his dad, Captain Denzel Cole say at times like these, when the enemy was bound to win, all your comrades would be dying or dead, and nothing you could do would change anything ...

"I appreciate the gesture," said Snow's mom, "But I have already claimed that one. There is no need for another."

Her words a frigid dagger in his heart.

"Then victory is assured," said Gordack. Coming closer.

When a loud wet crack erupted.

Then a huge bulk flew over Ash.

Over Snow's mom.

And crashed into a heap a few feet before her.

"Ash La Puska," said Felix. His voice rough, strained, but still full of power.

Coming from where the crack erupted.

Snow's mom whipped around.

A flash zipped over Ash.

"Drink the final –" began Felix.

Then a thump.

Snow's mom no longer had a sword.

But Ash's pocket was now empty.

Just like the small flask with no more liquor.

CHAPTER

TWENTY-THREE

ASH, THE DRUNKEN AVENGER

The Final Chug burned all Ash's insides raw.

Turned the whole night sky from pitch dark to bright violet. Filled with milky stars. Hazy white glittery mist.

The cobble beneath his back jabbing him. Jagged pokes against bruised ribs and spine. The chills washed away with burning sweat.

The lampposts still dim but now more than clear. Their artistic curve. The walls, despite being splattered by blood, clearly depicted the fruits and fun this city was meant to be. The splashing wine that should be the only liquid staining the stone walls. The broken boards from hawker stalls as unwelcome a sight as the corpses collapsed over shredded ratty mats.

As unwelcoming as all the shuttered windows all completely dark. The doors closed and obviously barred and locked form the other side. The residents shivering, utterly silent, hoping the darklings outside wouldn't shattered their flimsy wooden defenses.

Wouldn't add them to the corpse count.

The fact that the Darkest Fourth still stood here. linger at this very spot. The exact extent if this darkling's power unknown, for the last Darkest Fourth in the last war had destroyed whole kingdoms through enslaving the rulers through perfumes and evil counseling, counseling the forced barbaric games whose natures were never spoken of, even now, in the grim hope they would be forgotten, they wouldn't ever be repeated.

Right now, the Final Chug demanded he stand up. Boot on cobble. Shoulders tall.

And draw his saber.

Fight for those who were now corpses around him.

Save all those civilians trapped inside the maze of buildings. Hidden by Snow at the cost of her life. Given a chance to live by Felix's determination to slaughter as many of the invaders as possible.

Even crush their commander general at the cost of his own life.

Ash no longer needed the lampposts to see. The milky moonlight might as well have been sunlight at noon.

The fiery liquor inside him powered Ash to his feet. Boot on cobble. Shoulders tall.

Saber drawn.

Because any decent soldier knew what they had to do now.

Even if Ash was never a decent soldier, his duty burned

through his blood like fiery acid. Flaming at the fact Felix and Connie deserved to live far more than he ever did. Of all the people to die last, Ash wasn't the one meant to survive. In fact, everything he did was practically a death wish.

And now his saber would deal death to a certain lycan who so richly deserved it.

Yet the Darkest Fourth merely sneered at him.

Pointed her claws at him.

Ash charged at her. His boots pounding the cobble. Cracking it. Each step a swift zip closer.

Till only steps away.

"A strength empowerment," said the Darkest Fourth, "Pathetic."

Then turned her palms up. Fingers up. Her jasmine stink all too clear.

Ash's blade pointed at her chest. Ready to rip through that blackest of hearts.

Only two steps away.

"Arclight," she said.

The world sizzled. Baked like the air in an overheated oven. Tingled like the touch of a bronze door knob after walking too long on a scrappy wool rug. His whole body tensing for the inevitable strike of deadly magic.

Yet nothing struck.

Until Ash lunged that last step.

A crack and a swoosh.

She gasped when he pressed the blade against her throat.

"Can you revive them as they were?" asked Ash. His voice so quiet for the raging currents roaring through him

The gape of shock. Her stiff pose.

"I –" she stuttered.

"Then die," he said.

"Wait!" she cried. Falling backwards. Bump. Right on her evil rear. Palms up above her shoulders. "I surrender! I'll swear to be your purren! Just –"

Ash pressed his blade against her throat again.

"Swear to speak the honest truth," he said.

"I swear to –"

"A proper oath!"

"I, Jasmine Winters, swear to speak the honest truth to you," she said, "And serve as your devoted, loyal, and faithful purren for life if you spare my –"

"You murdered your own daughter!" he said, "Can you revive her and my other companions as they were. Yes or no?"

The raw bitter fear coming off her answered Ash's question right away.

Until a chuckle rang out behind him.

"She can't," said a voice as creamy evil as milk mixed with blood, "But *I* can."

ASH SWUNG AROUND. Cracking the cobble again. The patter of blood on his boots wrenching his insides at the knowledge of whose it was, of what could of been if he had put the obvious pieces together quicker.

Hadn't been too drunk from all the liquor to recognize Snow for who she was.

To guess the vandread Amber was likely some kind of copy. A genuine copy, probably, but a copy, nonetheless.

The taps of the Darkest Fourth running away clear in the new silence. Her stink, her wyrming namesake even, still fouling the humid air. The tall walls cramped like a deep tunnel echoed those claws scratching the street, scratching her ears with his idiocy. A corridor within a deep chasm, filled with a roaring river of bitter regret, as bitter, as sour, as whole bottle of priceless wine vinegarized, then mixed with the finest of ales turned very, very bad.

The dark sky overhead, with its glittery milky haze, not a sprinkle of hope.

And the new enemy was definitely far worse.

A dozen feet beyond Ash. Centered between the vandread Amber's body and a brightly painted wall. Right between two lampposts. Civilian corpses nearby.

Not even Snow's spells could of hid the survivors here. Not behind closed shutters or doors. Without a single light on.

Because here the darkness would only turn against them. The way every bit of darkness here swirled about, so subtle, like a bit of translucent cloth caught on a twig deep in a silent yet rapid stream.

Because there stood the tall gaunt wizard that called himself the Soul Magus.

Pale deathly skin. A body of wiry brawn that dared try to match Felix's. His chest bare except for a crisscross of black leather and a huge ruby implanted in the center. His trousers and buckle as dark as his darks.

Black coals within a cruel arrowhead face and fiery red spike of hair.

And the monster titled the Darkest Third.

The Soul Magus jerk his right palm up. The stink of the dankest mausoleums, then of makeshift graveyards after a heavy rain, suddenly fuming the night.

And Felix clambered to his feet.

Except his eyes ... a black oily goo spewed out and formed two small smacking mouths. Both too much like grotesque misplaced antenna.

"The rest of the city," the Soul Magus said, "All those who have died."

He jerked his left palm up."

A scrap rang out behind Ash.

He leapt away.

Now Gordack stood. Looming his nine feet. With only his black fur on him.

Except for the saber protruding from his chest. A Paladin blade that could cut through anything easily. Now slowly sinking down to the ground, cutting through dead flesh that quickly knit itself back together.

And that same black goo antenna mouths out of his eyes.

"They all will join Felix and Gordack as my newest creations," said the Soul Magus, "As will you, Ash La Puska, when you die."

Gordack slashed his massive claws at Ash.

He ducked. Sliced off the limb at the forearm.

A clean cut.

Then jumped back. Cracking the cobble hard. Clearing a few feet away.

Except the cut ... the forearm and arm were now connected by an extension of black goo.

Gordack attacked with both claws now.

Paladin training, grinding thinking response into unthinking instinct, now unclear on the next response.

Ash hesitating a critical instant

Until Captain Cole's training kicked in. Training that covered unplanned, the uncovered.

In this case it might one thing – the ratling's huge size, get in close.

So Ash leapt in. Dodging the huge claws.

The cracks of Felix's boots nearby, a warning of his other enemy nearby. Perked his ears to listen harder. Listen for the swoosh of a blade, the crackle of fabric over swiftly moving body.

While Ash sliced through the ratling's thigh.

Then its side.

And tail.

The black goo rushed to connect them.

Its smell as biting as a blacksmith's furnace. With a few corpses thrown in for good measure.

Its sound as mushy as mushroom crushed together.

When the corner of his sight spotted Felix. That wall of dark brawn.

Ash ducked under the brawny fist.

Slicing it clean off.

The crush mushroom sound revealing the futility of it. The biting smell confirming it.

So Ash swerved around.

The Final Chug burning his body. Burning it away. Giving him strength to fight harder.

Faster.

And let him charge at the Soul Magus. Cobble shatter at every step. Wind battering his body, his clothes. Each split moment speeding him closer, closer, closer. The pale gaunt wizard sneering at the futile gesture. Hand wringing, uncaring.

The fire inside Ash burning away his life, definitely, for certain.

But some things were worth dying for.

When two roars ripped out from the side.

Two tentacles of rolling flames. Cracking against cobble and stone wall, consuming lampposts and corpses.

And directed by the old bag of wrinkled himself. Standing a few lampposts down from the Soul Magus.

But his eyes – the black goo antenna.

And whipped the flames at his son.

THE SHUTTERS THEMSELVES CRACKLING NEARBY. Shuddering at the heat, at the intensity of the winds. The walls chipping. Blood and paint peeling. Searing Ash's own mouth with a bitter coppery taste.

But not unlike the crazy obstacle courses Captain Cole

threw at his son. Full of random pits disguised with anything from branches to piles of ragged clothing, heaps of iron bars and rugged thorns to climb over, or swinging spiked logs, wobbly bridges, and worse.

Forget the ridiculous stuff during a Paladin's apprentice days. Like freezing one's ass off on mountain peaks. Where a team made a path through a wall of snow, where dry socks could make the difference between sickness and health, where drenched with too much sweat could kill, force some undressing and redressing regularly to prevent clothing from icing over.

Ignoring that extra magic involved. Detecting the subtle cracks and lines to signal where magic hid an entrance, a foxhole, or threads.

So a few good steps, cobble cracking even louder, and Ash dodged the worse of the flames.

Even if it seared his skin raw. Slowed his progress to a crawl. Stone slashing through his boots. Cutting his legs. Flame and flying rock ripping at his clothing, his flesh.

When a huge dark forearm grabbed his waist.

Another his free arm.

Then his leg.

Crushing them.

Dragging him back. Away from the Soul Magus.

Those black coal eyes as glinty evil as the blood red ruby on his chest. Its glint too bright for the milky moonlight. Its glow too clear in the darkness.

That smug smirk. Palms raised and ready to clench victory.

So Ash did what every instructor told every swordsmen never to do.

What no sane Paladin ever did either.

What even Captain Denzel Cole told him never to do.

But Ash was a drunk idiot at the core. The Final Chug was called final for a reason.

So he threw his saber. As hard as he could. Aiming it as best he could.

Which made the Soul Magus hesitate.

For a moment.

Long enough for the blade to plunge right through his ruby.

His howl cracked through the air. Cracked louder than the cobble did underneath Ash's boots.

And ended with his ruby shattering. The crackles splintering through the night itself. Causing the swirly darkling to suddenly stop. As if the rapid stream with the translucent cloth suddenly became a murky sluggish lake.

While the blade buried deep in his chest.

The black goo and the bodies it animated, the Earth Wizard, Felix, and Gordack, they all collapsed to the ground unmoving.

Freeing Ash again.

Another moment to finish this.

He charged. Only a few more steps. Only a couple before he could end this nightmare once and for all.

When he reached for his saber's hilt, still buried in the Soul Magus' chest. A single yank out, another swing could kill —

The Soul Magus snatched Ash's neck.

Squeezed tight.

Yanked him off the ground.

Lift him way above that cruel arrowhead.

So far above the torn gooey road, the shuttered window ruined, the walls with peeled paint and blood, the melted lampposts, and Ash's meek hand only able to clutch, to pointless pry against the Darkest Third's steel grip.

The stink of furnace fading from the stench of corpses. The heat of the night no longer so humid.

Starting to become cooler again.

Chilly.

The Soul Magus kept his long arm extended. Keeping Ash far away. So far he couldn't hope to deal a finishing blow, a strike at that arrowhead head, even if he wished to, even if he had the strength to.

Not with his fists at least.

Those thick arms of his enemy held more than enough muscle to default anything Ash could pound at it.

"You will die slowly for that," said the Soul Magus, "To delay my plans ... I will make you into a best creation yet. One that will rival all of Chemarin's corpses together!"

Ash's legs already trembled, as if gushing fumes from the Final Chug running out of fuel. His feet wobbled even worse than his knees. Even a kick to his shoulders would require too much effort at this rate.

The muscles packed thick, broad, and hard there, it could easily deflect the shredded boot anyway.

Not much strength left for anything. Maybe two serious blows.

If that.

Better make them count.

"Even ... Amber?" rasped Ash. Not bothering to use her correct name, Snow. Not reveal he figured out the truth.

Since if she were alive, was in his place, she'd scheme up a clever plan at this point. A completely complicated bizarre plan that in the end seemed completely obvious.

A good finale, as Amber insisted, always needed an impossible victory. A hard task. Even for a talented playwright like Amber. Easier to go with tragedy. Kill off everyone. Yet plausible but impossible success ... unrealistic no matter how you put it.

Yet it was always much more inspiring.

Especially outsmarting the brawny brain villains.

Ash, unfortunately, wasn't as clever.

Or quick thinking.

"The vandread," said the Soul Magus," A useful trap."

"Really?" asked Ash.

"A trap," said the Soul Magus, "That was all."

The Soul Magus refused to bring his arm closer. Let Ash see that victorious sneer up close. Prevented Ash from striking at his head.

Right now his boots might reach his chest wound. But the saber was already buried in as deep as it would go. It wouldn't slid down while the Soul Magus had enough strength left to magically counter the blade's edge.

So a solid random kick there, or anywhere on his torso, would do much good right now.

"A pretty amazing trap," said Ash, "She was just as clever, creative, and crazy as the real thing. It ..."

His tongue tripped his mouth. All because his dizzy wobbly head couldn't keep up. His skin decided to blister, scream in pain didn't help either. A body fried to a crisp ... well, he wasn't finding another fight anytime soon.

His vision was so bad by now he could barely make out the chipped painted wall behind the Soul Magus. It did seem a bit too bright behind the wizard though. Very blurry too.

But the pale bastard's cruel sneer and coal eyes ... still visible. His pale brawn too. A bit blurry.

But visible.

"Was merely a trap," said the Soul Magus, "Built from a corpse killed by a lycan assassin. Mind and body."

"So ..." said Ash. The words stabbing his sharper than all the shards and claws in all of this dying city combined. "The vandread was a genuine duplicate of Amber? Did she even know it?"

The chuckle matched the evil grin reaching those dark eyes.

A chuckle so loud in the sudden silence.

"Exactly," said the Soul Magus, "A genuine duplicate of your lost beloved vixen. One that believed she was the original and thought she had been human. Thought she was dragged from the pits of hell. But that foolish vixen's soul wouldn't be worth the price her demon master would demand for it. A perfect copy, however, with the right memories, that required a much cheaper price. The original was unnecessary as long as the copy remained ignorant."

His body couldn't match the agony Ash searing his own soul. That he failed Amber twice. As the vixen Snow, and as a copy. Because a perfect copy of Amber was, in fact, Amber – or Snow, this name thing would soon get confusing. But still, he should have found a way to save her. Just like Felix and Connie.

Just like Penny.

Even that vicious nutcase Mandy.

Originality was overrated, as Amber always said.

Yet Ash could barely manage a whimper.

And the chance for two Ambers, well the original could keep the name Snow and the copy stick with Amber, they would of loved to compete against each other. In their own bizarre way. Two Ambers fighting over him – if his cheeks were already fried to an aching crisp unable to even feel the air, they would of warmed a bit.

"You're wrong," said Ash, "Amber would of loved knowing. Both of them. They –"

The Soul Magus squeezed his throat tighter.

"Fool," said the Soul Magus, "For all men have a weakness for the right beauty –"

"Exactly," said the Darkest Fourth. Her voice close and behind Ash. The tip of a blade jabbing his back. Cutting a touch into it.

Right behind his racing heart.

That jasmine stink returning with reinforcements of the all the corpses she was responsible for in this city. If so many lampposts nearby hadn't been destroyed by the undead wizard's flames, Ash probably could of made out the Soul Magus better against the all the peeling paint and blood that had peeled away from the stone wall.

The fat Ash could still feel the tip of the blade against his back, even though his body could no longer feel the chill, or the humidity, or the heat, or whatever the temperature of the night was tonight. The taste of biting copper in his mouth drowned out the aftertaste of the liquor that almost saved him.

Almost saved Chemarin.

If only he could sigh, but his lungs felt too weak to bother roughing up the horribly silent night before these two darklings little boastful rants of utter victory.

"Faking my defeat," she said, "So easy yet it fooled you completely. Now you both are utterly helpless."

The Soul Magus snarled at the vixen bitch behind Ash. Lowered him to better shield himself. The blade jabbing his back slid in a bit more as it got reoriented by its holder.

By Ash's calculation, the cobble was now a couple feet below his boots. Assuming he wasn't too far off.

Not a safe assumption. Backed by plenty of experience.

"Truly foolish, vixen," said the Soul Magus. Raised the palm of his free hand.

And a ball of black gooey flame swirled bigger and bigger above it.

"If your despair is sincere enough," he said, "I may revive you with a body befitting your ugliness."

Tentacles popped out, wiggling out of the black ball.

As Ash's sight suddenly grew darker. Blurrier.

Then moans erupted everywhere. Nearby. With sound of massive moldy mushrooms mushed together. And the same stink.

"Mercy?" said the vixen, "Ha! Only my daughter Scarlet has ever proved herself worthy of it. And you have not."

But the Soul Magus chuckled again. Louder. Deeper.

"You yourself haven't earned it either," said the Soul Magus, "Right Snow?"

"What? She's –" said the Darkest Fourth.

Then gasped.

And a scream. Cut off.

His sight black. His body numb.

Only enough energy left for one last desperate move.

Yet the blade vanished from his back. A crack ringing out a moment later.

"Ash?" asked the one voice he never expected.

Snow, her voice similar to her role as Amber, though.

And a tiny stream of extra energy burst through him. A despair hope.

"Holy shitwads," she said, "Ash, what happened to you? You look like a goat's ass after it prancing in a thorn patch while pooping every leap of the way. And that smell ... how in the hell do I smell you so well. Everything so well. I – holy fuckwads on a shitter. My body. It's covered in white fur. With blue highlights. And ears ... oh dear hell in a cell, I merged with that horrible fox lycan, didn't I?"

"More like returned to your real body, it smells like," said Mindy, "The bodies of the vandread and Snow are gone – see? Judging from your scent, your face's expressions, this new body matches you more than its previous owner's. So does the expression of your body. Maybe you need more time to remember things right ... I still expect you to stick to your purren –"

A huff rang out that could only come from Penny. The cracks of her boots coming closer.

One last chance.

One quick calculation.

A guess. A gamble. Double or death.

"Okay, more importantly," said Penny, "Why the hell are we suddenly alive? Perfectly healed too. Don't tell me the pale bastard about to kill Ash did it."

And everything he had left.

"Of course I did," said the Soul Magus, "So you could all kill your precious Ash slowly and painfully until I am satisfied. Then you all shall serve me properly for eternity as living undead –"

"Exactly," said the Darkest Fourth. Whose furry legs suddenly appeared behind the Darkest Third. As if an invisible mist suddenly lifted. Revealing the pale stone wall behind the Soul Magus was, in fact, some kind of haze that now vanished, replaced by a dark stone wall painted and splattered with blood and peeled paint.

The tension in the Soul Magus' chest – likely some sword was in her hand. Its blade pointed right at her rival's heart, probably.

And gave Ash the moments gather his strength for one last strike. A double whammy.

A quick desperate move.

"Faking my defeat twice, faking an oath," she said, "So easy yet it fooled you completely. Now you both are utterly helpless and my minions, my own daughter lives again."

A gamble.

"Really?" asked Ash, "That's a relief."

Then nailed the Soul Magus' groin with his right boot.

Powered with all the fire left in his body.

The Darkest Third howled a squeaky squeal. Every bit of horrible smoothness in his voice gone. Shredded with any dignity the evil bastard might of had left with this victory.

A second kick, powered by every last bit of his inner fire's fumes, and Ash slammed the Soul Magus back into the Darkest Fourth.

Freed himself of his grip.

While she screamed. Till cut off by her rival's bulk smashing into her.

Turning into a bloody gasp.

So the blade through the now shattered ruby had cut all the way through both of them.

Good.

Only the gaunt wizard's magic kept it from sliding down before. But not now, Down to his hips. Down to the hazard zone all males similar to humans had.

Cutting both the wizard and the lycan behind him, judging by their gasping screams.

Until they ended with a cough. Loud and wet.

Jackpot.

Ash fell. Crumbled against jagged cobble. His body positioned awkward. Too weak and aching to better itself.

The taste of this victory was a bit too charcoally and dry though.

Especially with his vision now completely dark. Even if the lampposts were light to full strength. With the moon adding its milky light. Or just throw in the sun for good measure. So what if it was nighttime? He could imagine the sun rising anytime he wanted to.

It didn't matter that he was dying charcoal. Never to see the sun again.

Or see the people behind those closed shutters light up with hope. With relief.

A fleshy thump erupted nearby. Certainly the Soul Magus. Dead. The saber must of pierced his heart. Putting the ruby in front of his weak point. Probably added some extra impossible to cut magicked metal around it for extra security ...

A classic mistake in plays.

But not in real life.

The best armor around the most important weakness? Common sense and practical in real life. So someone like him, focused on practical real-life stuff, would never consider broadcasting it a bigger weakness than armoring it up.

Nor would any normal fighter. Like Captain Denzel Cole.

Then more wet coughs erupted from the woman. Weaker. With moans. Sinking toward the ground. Stopping a bit later.

But not the stink of fresh blood.

Ash didn't need to guess the identity of the bitch.

"Mom?" gasped Snow, "Then who, when, a fox lycan?! Really? Since when was I ... don't tell me ... some soul leaping, merging, or whatever weirdness is messing with my memory ... ugh. Don't tell me I've got follow through with every oath I made during a play. No wonder lycan never appreciated –"

The Darkest Fourth growled. Wet and gurgling. Rasping. Too bad he couldn't see her expression. Add in some gloating for good measure.

"You useless idiot!" she rasped, "Falling for that human boy when you should of killed him! Your first mission as the Darkest Second, ruined, spoiled, by –"

"Wait, wait, wait!" exclaimed Leo, "Not quite right there. Yes, my Amber Honey, and my duplicate Snow merged with the original Snow, and you, Angela Snow, got fully kicked back into your original body. But ... what was I talking about? Oh yeah, I remember ... oh no. Oh yeah. Oh no. Oh – ACK!"

"So, Leo," said Snow. Her lycan growl very lycan.

Ash resisted the urge to congratulate her on it. Breathing was hard enough as it was. His whole body going numb – even the pain vanishing – not exactly as helpful as he would like. His verbal abilities couldn't be much better.

Meaning it was too late for a long decent deathbed soliloquy. Since if he was going to die at this point, might as well do it with style.

No. A quick catchphrase approach will have to do.

His mind blanking that instant – his sigh came out a rasp.

And he ran out of air for another raspy sigh when he realized he missed Amber's follow up to her lycan growl.

Sucking in more air proved slower and harder than it ever should.

Not many breaths left then.

"No worries, Amber Snow," said Leo, "That's your real name. Now you're in your real body again. So memories should be returning shortly and completely and very, very – ACK!"

Another very lycan growl from Amber.

Better leave a good deathbed catchphrase for the Amber in this world or else the duplicate Amber now in the next world would scold his ass off.

Or whatever get scolded off in the afterlife.

Yet he blanked again.

But didn't sigh afterwards.

Good. An improvement.

"Ash!" screamed Leo in his ear.

Ash jerked. Well tried to jerk. His body simply twitched. Sort of. Better than outright ignoring him.

Another improvement.

"I'll fix you up or a price," said Leo, "Throw in a few physical improvements. Like enhancements your durability. Maybe a few power ups. That sort of thing. In exchange, let's say you owe me a favor. Or two. Deal?"

From the intensity of the kitty bat's voice, the cat was defi-nitely sitting on his head. Probably resisting the urge to nibble and lick his sweet charcoaled body.

Both deserved some credit.

And Amber definitely negotiated this deal with her newfound – or newly recovered – lycan growls for help. So better not waste it.

Ash said yes. His throat emitted some gargled scratchy grunt.

Then refused any more air. In or out.

"Excellent!" said Leo, "Just close and eyes and go to sleep. When you wake up, you'll be all better."

His eyes were open?

What –

CHAPTER

TWENTY-FOUR

CAPTAIN DENZEL COLE,
STANDING STERN AGAINST DOOM

The never-ending chill in the crisp air preserved the crushed remains of Sir Isaac's skull. Even after three dreaded days, the Beast hadn't bothered to gather the shattered skull. Place it on another crude spike and add it to the gruesome fence four hundred yards away from the ridge.

And no one dared brave the deep holes or miniature ridges to fetch it for a proper burial.

Not even the shivering blond private whose dreams of the heroic Isaac were crushed so recently.

The eerie silence of the snow-capped mountains was far worse than the hallow windy howls that typically haunted Storm Killer. Every crackle and bang made by the captain's men echoed out everywhere. The groans of stomachs empty.

Too nauseous to eat their last breakfast of mushy oatmeal and cured bacon.

While the army beyond the curve in the pass remained silent and unseen. Only their horrible cry once they arrived over a month ago proved their presence.

But this tall ridge blocked the one and only usable passage through the mountains. Every man here was now stationed on top. Either with blades or bows. Their lycan pelts no longer could keep the cold from chilling them.

Keep them from visibly shivering.

Because the inevitable battle was about to begin.

The moment the Beast appeared. Challenged them to send their last Champion against it.

To crush their last hope.

The fence of skulls would certainly be destroyed today. Along with humanity's last hope of survival. The grey sky as gloomy as Captain Denzel Cole himself.

Even with the sun taunting them with enough light to see their own end.

The taste of their inevitable defeat as bitter as the wine turned vinegar, he forced his son to drink in the vain hope of breaking his terrible habit of overdrinking.

But his son was long dead. The lycan would of found and slaughtered him years ago.

Soon the captain would join the rest of his family in the afterlife.

Because the Princes already sent a message. No other champions remained except one. Currently, a Paladin named Felix. The greatest of his generation and too far to the south to ever hope to reach here in time.

Unless a wizard aided him.

Their only hope now.

Shattered when the dreaded inhuman roar broke out before the ridge.

The Beast emerged from a system of holes of ridges so deep it hid the massive ratman. A creature twice the height of the tallest of men. Brawn so massive lifting a stallion would be child's play. Even if it wore the sturdiest armor in all of the Four Realms.

It raised its curved claws high. Reminding everyone here those claws were like short daggers capable of stabbing through the hardest steel.

Its black fur groomed into sharp spikes larger and thicker than before. Its huge fangs gleamed in a sadistic grin.

And yet again, it's even blacker pants were clean and unwrinkled. Not a speck of filth on its crimson vest with golden spirals.

Not a sign of the blood and brains that splattered out of Sir Isaac's head three days ago.

On its back was its colossal battle axe. With the wilted yellow skull blade glaring over the Beast's shoulder.

But this time it was not alone.

An army of ratman swarmed out of the deep holes and ridges behind it. All smaller yet just as vicious. Their armor black and weapons huge. Each clanging as loud as their catcalls.

"Bring forth your last challenger!" exclaimed the Beast, "Do that and I grant you a few more moment for your menfolk to quiver in fear. For you woman to wail at their future fate as our slaves. And mourn your children before my kind roast and feast on them all!"

Captain Denzel Cole didn't speak. His throat clenching. Mouth drying.

Not even wine turned vinegar could taste so bitter.

The sudden silence of the next moment crushed him. Slid past as slow as an avalanche of gooey slime.

The Beast pointed up at Captain Denzel Cole. Matched by every beady eye of its rat army.

Then sneered wicked.

"Send that man down here," said the Beast, "I will grant your one and only leader left a chance to save his pathetic kind. The Princes ..."

The Beast sniggered. The looming peaks echoing the throaty dark chuckles even louder.

And amplified by every ratman behind it.

"They and their men fell quick to my apprentices," the Beast said, "As did the Earth Wizard and his Paladins in Chemarin. No Champions remain. No wizards. Just you and your pathetic ragtag –"

A bright flash blinded everything with pure white.

Yet vanished as quick as it appeared.

Revealing a new challenger.

WITHIN THE GRAY pass utter silence reigned supreme. As heavy and chilly as the air. With the stink of death fouled only by the stench of rat. So thick anyone even with the numbest of tongues could taste it.

Since the army of ratmen crowding the pass below might be one storm that Storm Killer might not kill.

Especially with the dreaded promise that even more dark-lings remained hidden in the deepest holes.

Yet the captain could only blink a few times at the sight of the newcomer.

A young man in the black suave coat and pants of a Paladin. Standing tall and proud nearly a dozen feet in front of the ratman. A saber strapped to his waist. His hair a black crow's nest.

A stark contrast to the three lycan females crouched behind the Paladin. An orange tigress that – from her pose and slight yet trained movements – experience told the captain she could cut down plenty of soldiers. Maybe even dodge the rain of bolts that would soon shower down from the ridge.

The two white vixens with blue highlights – clearly some kind of exotic bred at the pelt farms and somehow managed to escape alive.

Yet the three lycan positioned themselves like guards behind the Paladin. Not as his mortal enemies.

The ratman's gawk was frozen on its face. Just like his shocked brethren.

Until the Paladin spoke.

"So you want to face a real man?" asked the Paladin.

That voice ... Captain Denzel Cole gasped. Almost gasped. But his throat was so clenched it silenced him.

But not the pounding in his ears.

Or the razors shredding his insides over pending death of his dear son Ash. This army of ratmen wouldn't even leave a bone behind.

But none of the humans here would leave remained behind. These monsters could feast on their corpses till nothing was left.

The captain was sure of it.

"Any idiot with a sword could charge you. Or throw magic at you if they're a wizard," said Ash, "But let's duke this out the way only the toughest of men could ever dream of ... a way that kills lesser men simply for trying ... a way not even the greatest of Champions – or darklings – could handle ... can you?"

If the captain could speak, he'd scream out a warning. Point out the glimpses of the fence of skulls was all from champions crushed by the monster before him. Even if it was now mostly hidden by these darklings.

In the utter silence his voice would reach his son. Give the boy a sliver of a chance to prepare.

The Beast blinked.

Its brow furrowed.

Then snorted.

"Bring forth this 'impossible' challenge," said the Beast, "And when I crush you, you will kneel and despair as I kill slow and painful. Then destroy the rest of your kind."

Then the Beast waved its hand at the fence of spiked skulls. His henchmen moving aside to reveal it.

"Then add you to my lovely collection," it said.

"Fine by me," said Ash, "Ending as a work of art ... not the worst thing possible."

Captain Denzel Cole couldn't help but gulp. His dry mouth crackling.

What was the foolish boy thinking to say that?

Ash reached into his pants pocket and slipped out a steel flash.

"First one to finish downing this flash and remain standing wins," he said. Then swing it up. Chugged down two gulps.

Then released a sigh.

A burp.

Then tossed it to the Beast.

Who caught it easily.

Its expression as scornful as the captain's own whenever his dear idiot of a son tried to drown his problems with alcohol and inevitably failed. The harsh whispers from the darkling army – they would slaughter everyone here in the worst ways possible.

"I suggest only one sip at a time," said Ash, "Maybe two if you're brave enough."

But the Beast snorted again. Its eyes now deep bloody red.

Enough to sink the captain's heart down to his knees.

"Liquor?" asked the Beast, "Such a pathetic game."

"Then finish it," said Ash, "But don't say I didn't –"

The Beast throw the whole flash in its mouth. Crunched it apart and gulped it down.

And chuckled.

"I will salvage your lycan body guards for this," said the Beast. Wrought its claws at them.

Its huge body looming higher. Arched and marching toward the fool of a boy. The claws on its feet scrapped the hard rock loudly.

A countdown for the end of humanity.

And all Captain Denzel Cole could do was grip his blade ever more tightly. Wait for the rest of the ratmen army to charge.

To break the ridge that would soon no longer hold the name Storm Killer.

"Their female bodies ... especially the Ivy Reap's," said the Beast, "They will bear some of my young before I roast you and your lycan aliiive –"

The Beast stumbled. Its foot landing on the ground yet its legs acting as it if it missed.

A snarl erupted louder than any creature before it.

"What kind of poison is this?!" shrieked the Beast, "I am immune to all those pathetic deadly tricks!"

"Not poison," said Ash, "Just liquor so powerful it's called the Final Chug."

The boy might as well kick his father in the gut. That legendary liquor literally killed the people who drank it. Only the sturdiest of alcoholics managed to survive more than a few gulps. Most men passed out drunk merely from breathing the fumes too much.

Yet the soldiers on the ridge ... their shoulders no longer drooped.

The ratmen ... their faces now tense and jittering.

"You ..." growled the Beast.

And stumbled again. Falling to its knees several feet before Ash.

Then lunged at him.

"Die!" screamed the Beast.

Yet Ash didn't move.

No.

The orange tigress flew at the ratman. Grabbed the arm of the massive monster. Twisted and turned her lithe body. Ramming herself into it.

Flipping the ratman over Ash.

And the Beast crashed into the ground behind the boy. Gurgling and choking. Struggling to climb to its feet.

Blood pooling beneath it.

When the Beast shuttered.

Then collapsed.

A few moments later, every soldier on the ridge cheered louder than any army of darklings.

The ratmen edged back. Eyes wide. Despite their thick black armor, their huge weapons lowered.

When a new roar erupted behind Storm Killer.

And the screams united as one shout of darkling doom.

ABOUT THE AUTHOR

Widely traveled, Jonathan Evan Hudson spends as much time studying life as he does writing gripping tales of fantastic adventures. From the giant redwoods of California to the deserts of Israel, his thrilling stories all draw on first-hand experiences and expand them with the fantastic and his acclaimed creativity.

Be the first to know!
For the updates and more:
www.JonathanEvanHudson.com

youtube.com/@jonathanevanhudson
tiktok.com/@jonathan.evan.hudson

A War Of Lust And Oak

Read Now!

The Elf Girl Effect

Read Now!

The acclaimed Jonathan Evan Hudson once again weaves an unforgettable tale brimming with spicy page-turning action and fast-burning enemies-to-lovers passion.

Meet the newly knighted Roo Vorshaya. Sworn to protect humanity in the isolated mountain town of Appleharth. Dreams of action-packed adventure and passionate love under a lovely but sinister strawberry-pink sky.

Love re-ignited by a whiff of the familiar peaches and cream scent of his long-lost childhood girlfriend: the notorious elven witch Amber Peaches.

And endangering everything Roo holds dear.

Love page-turner novels of epic fantasy? Love reading from dusk to dawn? Then go read *The Elf Girl Effect* now!

Martial Art Of The Phantom Saber

Read Now!

Succubus Slash

Read Now!

The acclaimed Jonathan Evan Hudson weaves an unforgettable tale of thrilling action and adventure spiced with fast-burning romance and doused deep in epic fantasy.

Enter Miles Mayhem. Rich in friends and enemies. And a fat boy badass in the sword.

A seriously delicious smell of bacon and eggs smothered in spiced razor-hot cheddar signals celebration—and serious trouble ahead.

Trouble beyond anything Miles ever expected.

The perfect epic fantasy novel. A genre-enlarging feast for fans of sexy action and fabulous adventure. Read *Succubus Slash* now!

Sword Master Of Honey Heart Resort

Read Now!

Into Shadow Forest

Read Now!

A diamond in the rough the bestselling Jonathan Evan Hudson weaves a thrilling tale from explosive beginning to satisfying end in the awe-inspiring land of Grandcrest.

The talented twenty-something sword master Romeo Bladell yearns for love and adventure.

And at the musty edges of Shadow Forest. Near the towering high oaks bearded like stout old dwarves. By a canyon like a wound gnashed deep through in the granite. A canyon like the maw of a stone dragon.

A strange unexpected rope bridge hangs silently. Sinisterly.

Beckoning adventure—and danger unimaginable.

Enter *Into Shadow Forest* and savor the most spectacular of page-turning epic fantasy novels. Love unique monsters, riveting battles, and fantastic femme fatales? Then read *Into Shadow Forest* now!

Angels Of The Sword

Read Now!

Crossing Of Shadowed Death

Read Now!

The acclaimed master of fantasy Jonathan Evan Hudson once again shines through with his talented story-telling. Time to enter another stunning awe-inspiring world of dangerous demons, magical mayhem, and action-packed adventure.

A simple demon-hunting mission. The young and lonely Dirk yearns for amazing adventure, for gorgeously under-dressed dancer girls among the towering high ferns. Among the even taller pines of the hot and humid Fern Shadow Forest.

Pine needles everywhere. And so fragrant they made the finest of teas.

Sturdy reliable cobble roads of the Divine Empire cut through the whole entire forest. Providing the only safe passage.

Or so Dirk thought …

Enjoy this sexy, action-packed epic fantasy adventure from the talented Jonathan Evan Hudson. Love to read an enthralling epic fantasy novel full of stunning rip-roaring battles with creative new monsters? Then go read *Crossing of Shadowed Death* now!

A TASTE OF INTO SHADOW FOREST

A diamond in the rough the bestselling Jonathan Evan Hudson weaves a thrilling tale from explosive beginning to satisfying end in the awe-inspiring land of Grandcrest.

The talented twenty-something sword master Romeo Bladell yearns for love and adventure.

And at the musty edges of Shadow Forest. Near the towering high oaks bearded like stout old dwarves. By a canyon like a wound gnashed deep through in the granite. A canyon like the maw of a stone dragon.

A strange unexpected rope bridge hangs silently. Sinisterly. Beckoning adventure—and danger unimaginable.

*Enter **Into Shadow Forest** and savor the most spectacular of page-turning epic fantasy novels. Love unique monsters, riveting battles, and fantastic femme fatales? Then read **Into Shadow Forest** now!*

CHAPTER 1
ROMEO

Romeo Bladell knew there shouldn't be a rope bridge crossing the canyon here yet ...

Here it was.

And the canyon itself was a deep jagged gash in the granite. Actually, more like how the maw of a deep gray dragon was.

(Not that he'd ever seen a dragon of any sort, but maybe one day ...)

The canyon itself was only a few good times wider than he was tall—but he wasn't exactly tall, and now that he was in his late twenties, it was long past the time where he'd get any taller.

The posts the ropes were tied to were stout logs. They only went up to his knees, but they still reminded him of his stout dwarven grandpa, whose bald head, even when he was on his toes, could only reach the tips of Romeo's chest.

But ... the logs looked older than some of the thick craggy oaks behind him. You know, the kind of oaks so old the moss of them doubled as old guy beards.

No, dwarf beards.

The planks were light gray and as warped as the weird joke the world had to be playing on him. The occasional gust of wind was refreshingly cool, like a lemonade during a hot summer day—like today actually, it was hotter than a hot spring with a roasting rock tossed in, so the gusts were more than welcome.

Each gust also made all four ropes of the bridge crackle out as loud as the crows in the bearded oaks behind him.

The bridge was even sunken a bit by the middle.

Like a sly bridgy smile—at the joke being played on him.

He was a lean and mean five foot six, so yes, he was a bit on the short side, for a human, but compared to dwarves, he was on the taller side, and he was muscular enough to wear his red jerkin like a vest, with no shirt, and his brown slacks were snug, but not tight.

Rather than risk another pair of flimsy sandals breaking again, he went with his reliable suede boots. They were dark red and the darkness was not entirely from the dirt of use. They were like thick reliable socks. Thick enough to protect his feet yet he could still easily feel the soggy soil underneath them.

Feel the few smooth pebbles in the soil.

Maybe climb down the canyon but ... the sides of the canyon were steep cliffs. At the bottom it would be incredibly slippery. It would take another hour or two. No. More like three. Assuming the light lasted. Longer if it didn't.

Much longer—and for what?

His backpack was basically a big bag with shoulder straps. It was made from sturdy burlap but far from water proof. It had some long-awaited precious books—more than a few of those books were the latest dime dreadfuls meant for guests, but he got to read them first to ensure there weren't any obvious problems. There were more than a few bottles of absolutely needed olive oil for lamps and cooking. Most important of all, some general provisions for the next few days.

Get the provision wet ... and not just the books ... yikes.

But Romeo ... the hackles on his neck stood up just looking at the odd bridge. It seemed to promise the hope of saving him over two hours. The usual bridge was an arch of stone along the paved usual road, but it crossed the river below long after the canyon was no longer a canyon.

And that bridge was well over another few hours hike away.

This shortcut, hiking along the canyon already saved him a few hours since the regular road made a very wide curve around the forest behind him.

All because rumors of monsters in there, but they were just rumors. Yup. Still, the bearded oaks behind were a part of the fringe of what was known as Shadow Forest and he had seen some of the corpses of the beasts in there ... like horse-sized blue jays called jumping raptors and ...

No.

They and the other dangerous beasts were only found

much further south, much deeper in the forest, not here, in the fringes, at the edge of the civilized world.

In fact, that hint of danger was a draw to the Honey Heart Resort. Honey Heart Resort was a spring bath inn and resort on top of the mountain here where Romeo was working at for the past few years.

Sigh.

So as Uncle Jethron would say, trust your nose when all else fails, and Uncle Jethron was among the best trackers in the county—human and dwarf.

So ...

CHAPTER 2

ROMEO

... **S**niff. Sniff.

The smell ... earthy soil. Mossy oak like all forests everywhere. The cool crisp clean smell of the river below. Echoes of the splashes and crashing of foamy rapids splashing against unyielding rock. Echoes snapping against the canyon's steep sides.

The usual smells. Sounds.

The midday rain had washed away his own footsteps from the morning trip. The crazy heat had already dried out the soil enough for it not to be outright muddy.

Just damp.

In fact, the wooden posts showed the usual expected grim from the ages.

You'd think the bridge had been here for ages too.

But it hadn't.

This very morning, on the way to town, back when the taste of his latest experimental pine needle tea was burning his mouth far too bitter, there hadn't been any rope bridge here at all.

Along the cliff on the other side of the canyon, the lichen showed no scraps along the jagged rock cliffs—no sign of any climber involved in setting up the bridge.

And Romeo read enough books over the years to know what's involved.

Rope would of been secured on one side of the canyon, and the climber climb down, go cross the foamy rapids by jumping the slimy slippery rocks, and climb up and stake the ropes on the other side.

In fact, Romeo had done such work as a side job here and there.

Another, more straightforward approach was to shoot arrows with rope tied to the ends into one of the trees beyond the canyon. Someone else on the other side would then tie the rope to the post.

Or if a heavier rope was needed, only a lighter rope would be shot and secured to the trees on both sides of the canyon. The thicker rope would be carried over and tied to posts on each side.

But ... no matter how much Romeo studied the line of bearded craggy oaks on the other side, there wasn't a sign of torn moss, of any arrows shot into their bark, or even a sign that the dirt was disturbed in the slightest.

Looking up at the sky, mostly blue with some clouds, but ... less than a few hours to sunset.

Legends said monsters were most active after night, and this close to Shadow Forest ...

Getting to the road ... he might not make it back in time.

Aunt Tilda would. be. *pissed.*

She was as big as ma, being her older sister and all, and she was the kind of women a guy would sprint a few laps around, as a woman should be, would be what pa would say, and grandpa, but ... ugh.

He really to get back before sundown.

Aunt Tilda was the boss lady of Honey Heart Resort, and he knew there were more than enough provisions for the night. For the next morning ... enough. Aunt Tilda could scrap enough together to last a couple more days but ... sigh.

Lucky for him it was Tuesday, not Monday. Tuesday was the slowest time of the week, even now, during the peak of summer, the hottest and busiest season.

But Romeo also knew this path wasn't commonly taken. Few even knew of it. Most travelers would take the long winding road rather than risk whatever trouble the fringes of Shadow Forest may throw at them. Rumors of monsters and worse things ...

Sigh. Would Aunt Tilda believe him about this bridge?

Even if she did, she'd absolutely forbid him from taking any "short-cut" (or "long-cut" as she'd call it then) off the road ever again.

(One sister and his foolish hubby lost was enough, she'd say, she wasn't about to risk her dear nephew, the last of her flesh and blood ...)

And ... honestly, it's unlikely anyone else would even run

into this rope bridge. No other witnesses. This place was so ...
empty ... so ... weird ... weird place for a trap but deep down ...

WANT MORE?

Go to

WANT MORE?

Go to

www.JonathanEvanHudson.com